20p

'I think you n
own medicine
Sean growled.

'Oh, is that a fact?'

shrug. Her smile was just the tiniest bit smug as she looked into his passion-darkened eyes. 'Is that a threat or a promise, Dr Fitzgerald?'

'Either…both…whatever…you…want…it…to…be!' He punctuated each word with a kiss then grinned as he saw the effect he'd had. 'Make up your mind.'

HEARTBEAT

LOVE** WHEN **LIFE** IS ON THE **LINE

In the intense atmosphere of the Emergency department, dedicated medical professionals race against time to save patients' lives.

But can these men and women also find fulfilment in their own lives – and in each other's arms?

Lives lived heartbeat to heartbeat...

This special collection of sixteen books from some of Medical Romance's most exciting, emotional and intense authors offers you a glimpse into the life, love, passion and caring of the Emergency department.

All the characters in this book have no existence outside the imagination of the author, and have no relation whatsoever to anyone bearing the same name or names. They are not even distantly inspired by any individual known or unknown to the author, and all the incidents are pure invention.

First published in Great Britain 2000. This edition 2004.
Harlequin Mills & Boon Limited,
Eton House, 18-24 Paradise Road, Richmond, Surrey, TW9 1SR

ISBN 0 263 84487 0

142-0304

Printed and bound in Spain
by Litografia Rosés S.A., Barcelona

HEARTBEAT

LOVE WHEN LIFE IS ON THE LINE

FOR BEN'S SAKE

Jennifer Taylor

MILLS & BOON®

CHAPTER ONE

'HELLO, Claire. Did you have a good holiday, then?'

'Lovely, thank you, Margaret. Two weeks of lazing around, doing nothing...bliss!'

Sister Claire Shepherd glanced back towards the waiting-room and grimaced. It was barely eight a.m. but already there was a queue of people waiting to be seen in the accident and emergency unit of Dalverston General Hospital. 'Mind you, from the look of the crowd out there, I'll be needing another holiday very soon!'

'You don't know the half of it. All hell broke loose the day after you went on leave. I don't suppose you've heard about Dr Carmichael yet?'

'No. Why, what's happened?' Claire let the staffroom door snap shut and went to her locker to put away her bag. 'I've only been off for a couple of weeks so I wouldn't have thought much could have gone on in that time.'

Margaret laughed. 'Oh, no? Well, try this for starters—Juliet Carmichael walked out of here the day after you went on holiday. And she won't be coming back.'

'She won't?' Claire couldn't hide her astonishment. 'Why on earth not?'

'Because she's had enough of trying to do the job of three people. Haven't we all? There's barely enough staff to cover at the best of times, and with the senior house officer's post still vacant it's put even more pressure on the junior doctors.' Margaret sighed. 'Juliet decided that she'd had enough and resigned on the spot. I believe she's thinking about giving up medicine altogether.'

'That's terrible! Such a waste of her training, too. The management are going to have to do something soon. We can't go on like this, not if it means staff walking out because they can't cope with the workload.'

Claire shut her locker then checked her watch. There were still ten minutes to go before they went on duty. She plugged in the kettle. 'Fancy a coffee?'

'Please.' Margaret went to the window, which looked out across the staff car park. 'Actually, I think it gave the powers that be a real shock, Juliet leaving like that—so much so that they've managed to find somebody to take over from her, at least on a temporary basis.'

'They have?' Claire spooned coffee into mugs then edged Margaret aside so that she could get the milk out of the fridge. 'That was quick. It usually takes ages to get a replacement, especially at this time of the year when everyone is after staff for holiday cover. Who is it? Do you know?'

'I've not seen him yet. He starts this morning. But Sally was here when he came to look round and her description was tall, dark and drop-dead gorgeous!' Margaret peered out of the window. 'And if I'm not mistaken, that's him now. He certainly fits the bill right enough!'

Claire smiled at the appreciative note in her friend's voice. She glanced out of the window and felt the shock sear straight to the soles of her feet as she saw the man who was walking towards the building. She closed her eyes, feeling her heart thundering inside her. It couldn't be him, not here. It was just someone who looked like him…

'What's his name?'

Her voice sounded whispery thin but Margaret appeared not to notice anything amiss. 'Fitzgerald, Sean Fitzgerald. Sounds Irish, don't you think?'

'I...I suppose so.' Claire opened her eyes, knowing there was no hope now that she'd made a mistake. The sun was behind him, casting his face into shadow, but she could remember his features so clearly that she didn't need to see them: those laughing deep blue eyes under strongly marked black brows; the nose with that hint of a crook in it, a souvenir from a childhood fight with one of his boisterous brothers; that lazy, devastating grin which had always turned her insides to water...

'Claire? Are you OK?'

'What? Oh, yes, just daydreaming. I'll make that coffee.' Claire managed a smile as she heard the quizzical note in Margaret's voice. She ran a shaky hand over her hair to smooth a dark red strand back into the heavy knot at the nape of her neck as she went to the kettle. She rarely wore her hair loose any more, preferring to keep the rippling mass of waves severely confined. It was stupid vanity which stopped her having it cut—that, plus the memory of how Sean had loved to take the pins out and let it fall around her shoulders...

She put the kettle down with a thud, avoiding Margaret's eyes as she picked up the sugar jar. 'Are you taking sugar at the moment? Or are you still trying to do without it?'

'Just half a spoon. I know I shouldn't but I hate the taste of coffee without.' Margaret took the mug from her but her expression was still curious. 'Are you sure you're feeling all right, Claire? You went as white as a sheet just now.'

'I'm fine. Honestly. It's probably the shock of having to get up so early after two weeks of lazing around!'

Claire gave a strained laugh, relieved when Margaret seemed to accept her explanation.

'It's only too easy to get used to the good life, isn't it?' Margaret took a gulp of coffee then put her mug down. 'I'll just nip to the loo while I get a chance. From the look of that crowd out there, I mightn't get another opportunity for a long time.'

She hurried from the room and Claire breathed a sigh of relief as the door closed. She shut her eyes again, willing herself to control the panic she felt, but it wasn't easy.

What quirk of fate had brought him here? she wondered dully. If anyone had asked, she would have confidently said that this was the last place on earth Sean Fitzgerald would appear! On the rare occasions she had allowed herself to think about him, she had pictured him someplace hot and dusty—Africa, where he had been heading the last time they had met, or maybe Australia, which had been another place he had dreamed of working.

The world was too big to settle for one tiny bit of it, he'd always claimed, and Claire had believed him. She had never imagined that their paths would cross again. Now it felt as though the bottom had dropped out of her world as she realised the problems it was going to cause if he found out why she had refused to go with him.

'Hello, Claire. How are you? Long time no see, as they say.'

She recognized his voice at once and could have wept. Even now the memory of this man was so deeply ingrained that all it needed was a few soft words, but, then, there had never been anyone to replace him.

'Come on, Claire. I know it must be a bit of a shock, but it was a shock for me as well.' His tone was so harsh that her eyes flew to his face, and she was stunned to see the bitterness in his eyes. 'I had no idea you were working here when I accepted the post. It was only because someone happened to mention your name when I came to look round that I realised you were here, so there's no need to worry that I've engineered this.' He gave a sardonic laugh. 'I wouldn't be that much of a fool. God knows, you left me in little doubt that you weren't interested in seeing me ever again!'

That stung. She stared back at him, haunted by the memory of that last bitter scene—Sean's angry voice demanding to know why she had changed her mind, his scornful laughter as he'd put his own interpretation on her decision not to go with him…

She took a small breath to rid her mind of the memories. There was only one thing she had to think about now, just one *person* she had to think about.

'Hello, Sean. As you say, it was rather a surprise to learn you were going to be working here. But I'm sure we're both adult enough not to let the past get in the way of us working together.'

She gave a small shrug, as though the idea was of little consequence, as her eyes swept over him. Sean had been devastatingly handsome eight years before and maturity had simply added character to his clean-cut features, she realized. His thick black hair showed no sign of grey either, whilst his six-foot frame looked as lean and fit as ever.

Her first impression was that he hadn't changed at all, yet as he came further into the room she saw that there was a new reserve in his blue eyes which hadn't been there once, a cynicism about the way he smiled which made a shiver dance down her spine.

'Why should it? That's all water under the bridge

now, isn't it, Claire? Both our lives have moved on in the past few years. I'm surprised you even remember my name.'

The taunting note in his deep voice brought the colour to her face. Claire forced herself to meet his mocking blue stare even though she could feel her stomach clenching with apprehension. Sean had no idea why she should have such good reason to remember him, and he must never find out! Her life was settled now and that was the way she wanted it to remain…for everyone's sake.

'Of course I remember you. Why shouldn't I?' She gave a light laugh, feeling the quiver which ran through her as he sat down on the edge of the table. Her hands clenched because the urge to reach out and touch him was so strong that it was hard to resist, but she couldn't allow her defences to drop even the tiniest bit.

'It wasn't all bad, was it, Sean? We did have some good times, as I recall.'

He gave a soft laugh but there was a depth to it which made her tense. 'So that's how you remember what we had, is it, Claire—a few good times to look back on?'

She looked away from his mocking face, knowing that she wasn't proof against what she saw there. Yet what did she see? Contempt? Certainly. But underneath there was something else, something that had the power to turn her life upside down if she let it. She didn't want to see regret in Sean's eyes and wonder what had caused it.

'Yes, if you want the truth!' she said sharply, to cut off that train of thought. 'That's exactly how I see our…' She stumbled over the word and Sean gave another laugh, softer still, yet the tiny hairs all over Claire's body seemed to lift in response to it.

'Relationship? Is that what you're finding so hard to come out and say? I don't know why. After all, that's what we had, Claire, a relationship...in the fullest sense of the word.'

She swung round abruptly because she couldn't bear to stand there and hear him taunt her with what they had once been to each other. She stared out of the window, focusing on the hills beyond the town. The view was one she loved, but suddenly it seemed alien, unfamiliar. It wasn't the view she used to see from the flat they had shared...

She took a quick breath before she turned, unaware how defensive her stance looked to the man sitting on the edge of the table. 'Yes, we had a relationship, Sean—*had* in the past tense. But it ended a long time ago and I can't believe that you've spent the last few years pining for me!'

She gave a bitter laugh, feeling the pain the words evoked, hating herself for feeling it. She had given up any claim to him eight years ago so she had no right to feel like this, angry and jealous at the thought of the other women he had known since.

'Neither do I imagine that you've spent them pining for me.' His gaze was challenging as he stood up. 'Believe me, Claire, I'm under no illusions so don't concern yourself about that. I just thought it best that we cleared the air and got things straight from the outset to spare us both any embarrassment.'

He glanced round as he heard voices coming from the waiting-room, and shrugged. 'Sounds like things are hotting up out there so let's leave it at that, shall we? At least we both know where we stand now.'

He left the room, but for a moment Claire just stood and stared at the door before she picked up the coffee-mugs and took them over to the sink, aware that her hands were shaking. Sean had said that they knew where they stood, but he didn't know all the facts. The situation was nowhere near as clear-cut as he imagined it to be. His view could alter drastically if he found out what she had never told him.

She squared her shoulders as she turned on the tap. It was up to her to make sure that he never did find out!

'Now, Danny, just let me slip this over that bandage… There, how do you like that?' Claire smiled as the five-year-old boy held up his hand to admire the bright yellow finger stall she had put over the dressing on his right index finger. It was one of a new batch they'd got especially for the children and had a comical cartoon face printed on it.

'Boss!' Danny declared, his tear-stained face breaking into a huge grin. 'Wait till my friends see it!'

'Boss?' Claire laughed. 'Do I take that to mean you like it, then?'

'Course. That's what I said.' Danny gave her a look which spoke volumes about adults who didn't understand plain English. He wriggled down from the bed and shot out of the cubicle.

'Danny…Danny, you come back here!' His anxious mother gave Claire an exasperated look. 'No wonder he keeps having accidents! He's into everything from the minute he gets up in the morning to the moment he goes to bed. Only Danny would think of having his friends lift the cover off that drain to get his Action Man figure back, and then get his fingers in the way when they dropped it. I tell you, Sister, he'll turn my hair grey at this rate!'

'You must have your work cut out with him. He's

becoming one of our regulars,' Claire sympathised as she followed Mrs Graham from the cubicle. 'Now, do make sure you keep that dressing dry. If he's having a bath then put his whole hand inside a plastic bag and slip an elastic band round his wrist to keep it on. And you know that you have to take Danny to Outpatients next week, don't you, Mrs Graham? That's a very nasty injury and we'll need to keep a check on how it's healing.'

'Yes, I understand, Sister. That nice young doctor explained all that. He said something about Danny maybe needing a skin graft if the finger doesn't start to heal properly,' Danny's mother added uncertainly.

'That's right.' Claire smiled to allay the mother's fears. 'You saw for yourself that the top of the bone was showing through where Danny had sliced the tip off his finger. There's quite a lot of tissue missing and it's hard to tell if it will grow back at this stage. It might need a skin graft to help it heal properly. Hopefully, it won't come to that, but we'll just have to wait and see, as Dr…Dr Fitzgerald explained.'

Claire noticed her hesitation as she said the name. She glanced round as Mrs Graham hurried away to find her son. Sean was by the lifts, talking to an elderly woman in a wheelchair. As Claire watched, he bent down and patted the old lady's hand then laughed at something she said.

He had a way of putting the patients at their ease. Claire had noticed it at once despite the fact that she had been so tense. After a few words from Sean even the most agitated patient began to relax…

She turned away abruptly. Sean Fitzgerald was occupying far too much of her attention this morning! She had to start as she meant to go on, by thinking of him as just another colleague, difficult though that was going to be.

She took a look round the waiting area, inwardly groaning as she realized that the queue seemed as big as ever despite how hard they had worked. Most of the cases they had seen that morning had been fairly minor ones, though. No real emergency had come in, for which she was grateful. She could do with getting her wits about her before having to cope with a life-and-death situation.

The thought had barely crossed Claire's mind when Margaret poked her head round the corner. 'Paramedics coming in, Claire. ETA three minutes. Female, aged forty-eight, collapsed in the street, arrhythmic heartbeat. Her husband is with her.'

'Right. Thanks, Margaret. Can you go and check that everything is ready? I'll alert Dr Fitzgerald.'

She quickly made her way to where Sean was having a last word with the elderly woman before she was wheeled into the lift by one of the porters. He looked round as Claire quietly called his name, his face instantly losing its animation as he saw her.

'Yes, Sister? Do you need me?'

The chilly tone stung so that Claire replied just as coldly. 'Patient arriving by ambulance, Doctor. Collapsed in the street. Arrhythmic heart-beat. ETA approximately two minutes now.'

'Right. Is everything ready?' Sean made his way to the swing doors which led out to the canopied forecourt.

'Yes. Margaret is making a check on the trauma room.'

'Good. Ah, here they come, from the sound of it.'

Sean turned towards the gates as they heard the wail of a siren. Claire took a deep breath, forcing the hurt she felt at the way he had spoken to her so coldly to the back of her mind. Sean obviously intended to keep things on a strictly business footing, for which she should be grateful. Allowing herself to feel hurt was a foolish indulgence she couldn't afford.

'Hi, there, Doc...Claire. This is Helen Morris, aged forty-eight. Suddenly collapsed while out shopping. She'd evidently vomited before we got to her but nothing since. No history of cardiac problems but there are definite signs of arrhythmia.' Joe Henderson, one of Dalverston General's most experienced paramedics, started pushing the trolley towards the double doors.

'Thanks, Joe.' Claire bent and patted the woman's hand. 'Just take it easy, Helen. You're going to be fine. Try to breathe nice and steadily for me. That's right.'

She adjusted the oxygen mask over the patient's nose and mouth then turned to the ashen-faced man who had followed them from the ambulance. 'Are you Mr Morris? If you'd just go with the nurse while she takes some details from you, we'll try to get your wife sorted out.'

'Sh-she is going to be all right, isn't she! I just can't believe this. One minute we were walking along the street and the next...' His voice broke as he stared after the stretcher which was disappearing into the trauma room, a room that contained all the specialised equipment needed to deal with any kind of emergency.

'We'll do everything we can for her, Mr Morris,' Claire assured him. She nodded to Margaret, who came over and slid her hand under the distraught husband's elbow. 'Why don't you take Mr Morris into the relatives' room, Margaret? It will be quieter there.'

Leaving Margaret to deal with the necessary paperwork, Claire swiftly followed the patient. Helen Morris had been transferred to a bed now and Sean was bending over her, listening to her heart through his stethoscope.

'Did you experience any severe pain before this happened, Helen? Down your arms or around the base of your neck?' he enquired gently, removing the oxygen mask from the woman's face so that she could answer his questions.

'No. I felt fine. Then all of a sudden I began to feel sort of dizzy… Next thing I knew I was on the floor.' The woman's voice rose in panic as she clutched Sean's hand. 'I'm not going to die, am I, Doctor?'

'Not if I and the rest of the staff have anything to do with it!'' Sean gave her an encouraging smile. 'Something has knocked your heartbeat out of sync, Helen. It's a bit like trying to waltz to a rumba—the steps won't fit. We need to find out why it's happened and get things back to normal. Just try to stay as quiet as you can for me. Nurse Dawson here will connect you to the electrocardiograph so that we can monitor your heartbeat and see what's going on.'

He moved away from the bed as Helen closed her eyes, obviously reassured by Sean's easy manner. He nodded to Sally Dawson, who began attaching the electrodes to the patient's chest. His expression was thoughtful as he joined Claire at the foot of the bed.

'It's very odd. The patient is bradycardic her pulse is barely fifty at present. It apparently happened right out of the blue. She was violently sick and then fainted, although she'd felt fine until today. She hasn't suffered any dizziness or fainting spells in the past. Blood pressure is low, as could be expected. Once we get the ECG printout we'll have a clearer idea what's going on, but I suspect she's suffering from heart block. I think we need to give the cardiovascular registrar a call and get him down here right away.'

'Right away, Dr Fitzgerald,' Claire moved away to make the call, but not before she'd noticed the way Sean's mouth thinned at her use of his full title. She shrugged the thought aside by telling herself that he had laid down the ground rules and that she was simply following them. However, it didn't stop her feeling petty. All the staff worked so closely that first names were the order of the day and titles usually dispensed with...but, then, there was nothing 'usual' about this situation!

Claire put through the call, frowning as she was briskly informed that Brian Haversham, the senior cardiovascular registrar, was in surgery. She went back to tell Sean, who was watching the electrocardiograph's screen.

'Brian Haversham is in surgery. It's going to be at least an hour before he's free.'

'Damn!' Sean glanced at their patient. 'I would have liked to have got his opinion first. I'll give her a shot of isoprenaline to increase her heart rate but it's purely a temporary measure. She'll need monitoring to see what's going on. It could turn out that she'll need a pacemaker fitted, but it seems odd to me that she hasn't shown any symptoms before today, although it isn't unknown for that to happen, of course.'

'Maybe we should talk to Helen's husband and see what he can tell us?' Claire suggested. 'Although Helen claims that she's felt fine up till today, she may have overlooked something. At the very least he'll be able to tell us if there's a family history of heart disease.'

'Mmm, I was just thinking that myself. Two minds with but one thought, eh?' Sean teased, smiling at her. The smile seemed to light up his whole face so that

Claire felt her breath catch as she basked in the glow from it.

He turned away abruptly and his tone was once more brisk so that she had the impression that he regretted the brief moment of camaraderie. 'I'll just sort out that injection, then I'd like you to come with me, please, Sister. Mr Morris seemed very upset earlier. He might respond better if you're there when I talk to him.'

'Of course,' Claire agreed flatly, not trusting herself to say anything more. She took a deep breath as he moved away, wondering how she was going to cope in the coming weeks.

She was flesh and blood after all. She couldn't stop herself remembering how things had been once between them, even though she knew that, given the same circumstances, she would make the same decision. But Sean could never know what it had cost her eight years ago to let him go!

CHAPTER TWO

'NO, THERE'S nothing like that. Helen's parents are as fit as fiddles. We had a postcard from them only this morning, in fact. They're in Benidorm. Go there two or three times a year, they do, for the weather.'

Mr Morris rubbed a hand over his eyes. Claire shot a glance at Sean, who shrugged. So far it seemed there was little to suggest that Helen Morris's problems could be hereditary.

'Well, from the sound of it, Mr Morris, there doesn't seem any family predisposition towards cardiac trouble,' Sean admitted. 'How has your wife's health been generally? Has she had any problems which she's seen her doctor about recently?'

'No. But, then, Helen's a great one for home remedies, you see. She doesn't believe in going to the doctor.' Mr Morris frowned. 'I wanted her to see him a couple of weeks back but she wouldn't hear of it. Went into town, she did, and got something from that there herbal shop.'

'I see,' Sean said thoughtfully. 'And do you know what it was that she bought, or what it was for?'

'Well, it was something for these hot flushes she keeps having. But as to what it is she's been taking, I've no idea. Apart from that, there's nothing I can think of... Oh, except those herbal teas she's always drinking.' Mr Morris shuddered. 'Taste horrible they do. Our two boys call them Mum's witch's brews!'

Everyone laughed, which helped relieve a little of the

tension. However, Claire could tell that Sean was concerned by what he had learned. It didn't surprise her when he asked Mr Morris if there was any chance that his wife had the herbal medication with her.

'She might have. Here, let me look in her bag.' Mr Morris emptied the contents of a capacious handbag onto the coffee-table and began sorting through them. He gave a little exclamation of triumph as he held up a plastic bottle which bore the label of the local herbal emporium. 'Here you are, Doctor.'

Sean took it with a smile of thanks, turning towards the light to study its label. Claire frowned as she read what it said over his shoulder. 'Evening primrose oil capsules. Do you think they could be the cause of Helen's problem?'

'I don't think so. They are widely available and generally considered to be extremely safe. However, I'll have the lab run a check on them just to make certain they are what they claim to be. I'd also like to know what the overdose level is and what effects there are if it's exceeded.'

He sighed heavily. 'I'm certainly not against herbal medicine. However, the danger is that many people don't realize just how potent it can be. I've seen a number of cases where people have made themselves ill by taking an overdose.'

'Is it worth giving the herbalist a ring and asking him if there are any known side-effects from taking too many capsules?' she suggested. She shrugged when Sean glanced at her. 'I've been into the shop myself a few times and have always found him very helpful.'

'I think that's an excellent idea. Why didn't I think of it?' he demanded ruefully, with such a comical expression on his face that she had to laugh.

'Probably because you doctors are too used to having people running around after you,' she teased. 'We nurses don't have that luxury so we tend to be dab hands at finding short cuts to solve any problems!'

'Oh, that was below the belt, Sister!' His grin was infectious, so warm and friendly that her heart performed a small flip in response. Mercifully, he didn't appear to notice her reaction as he turned back to the older man.

'Well, we shall check these out, Mr Morris, just to be on the safe side. In the meantime, we're waiting for the cardiovascular registrar to see your wife. I've given her something to sort out the problem for now, but I'm sure he will want to keep her in for observation. However, she's in no immediate danger, I assure you.'

Sean looked at Claire again and she hurriedly smoothed her features into a suitably noncommittal expression. However, she couldn't help but notice the frown he gave before he continued. 'Sister will come back for you in a few minutes once I have taken another look at your wife. Then you'll be able to see her.'

'Thank you.' The man managed a smile. 'I know you're doing all you can but it's been such a shock.'

Sean clapped him on the shoulder. 'I know. But your wife is in the best place possible.'

He went to the door, waiting for Claire to lead the way from the room. However, once outside, he drew her into an alcove out of the way of anyone passing along the corridor. 'Are you all right, Claire?'

'Of course!' She heard the defensive note in her voice and blushed.

Sean sighed wearily. 'Look, it's going to be one heck of a strain for us both if we don't try to relax. I got the feeling that you were really on edge just now, and I hate to think that I'm the cause of it. I know this isn't the easiest of situations but we were always good friends above everything else, Claire. Do you think that somehow we could find our way back to being that again?'

His obvious sincerity brought a lump to her throat. That Sean had noticed her discomfort, even though he hadn't correctly interpreted the reason for it, thankfully, touched her. Yet why should it? Sean had always been caring and considerate. They had been two of the attributes she had loved most about him, and it seemed he hadn't changed in that respect. It was an effort to keep her tone level as she realised it.

'I hope so, Sean. I...I would like to think that we can be friends at least.'

'So would I, Claire.' His eyes darkened as they rested on her for a moment before he quickly turned away. Claire followed him back to their patient, her head in a spin.

Could she and Sean go back to being friends? Was it possible? He seemed confident enough but he didn't know all the facts. How would he feel if he found out the truth? Would he still want to be her friend then? Her heart slammed against her ribs because she already knew the answer to that question!

'Right, tea up! Sugar for you, Sean?' Margaret hoisted the big brown teapot off the worktop and started to fill the mugs.

'Two, please.' Sean grinned as he saw Margaret's brows rise. 'I know! You don't have to tell me—sugar is bad for you, it ruins your teeth, et cetera, et cetera. But give me a break. It's my one and only vice, I promise you!'

'I don't think!' Margaret laughed as she spooned sugar into a mug and passed it to him. 'I'm sure you have any number of far more interesting vices, Sean Fitzgerald! What do you think, Claire?'

Claire just smiled as she took the mug Margaret offered her, using that as an excuse to avoid replying. The crowd in the waiting-room had miraculously thinned so they were snatching a break while they had a chance. She sipped her tea, trying not to listen to the banter Sean and Margaret were exchanging. It only made her more conscious of the restraint between herself and Sean.

Apart from that brief interlude in the corridor, when he had suggested they try to resume their former friendship, Sean had continued to treat her with a rather distant courtesy. It was the best way, of course, but it didn't stop Claire feeling hurt when she remembered how they used to behave with one another...

'Come in, Claire... Are you receiving me?'

Claire jumped as Margaret's voice boomed in her ear. She looked up, the colour rushing to her face as she saw the look her friend gave her. 'Sorry, did you say something?'

'Oh, no! I've just been standing here having a conversation with myself for the past five minutes.' Margaret winked at Sean. 'Claire's just back today from her holiday. I don't know what went on but she's had her head in the clouds all morning. It must be love, that's all I can think from the way she's been mooning about!'

'Think so?' Sean took a sip of his tea. He smiled as he studied Claire over the rim of the cup, but she could see the glitter in his eyes even though she couldn't understand it's cause. Why should Sean look as though he was angry? she wondered hazily.

She shrugged off that thought, afraid of where it could lead. It would take so little to start looking for signs that Sean still felt something for her, but what was the point?

What they had felt for one another was over. She couldn't risk raking up the past because she had too much to hide!

She gave a light laugh, hoping that nobody could notice the panicky undercurrent it held. 'You know what your problem is, Margaret—you let your imagination run away with you! I had a nice, quiet holiday and that was it.'

'Typical! And here was I holding out great hopes, too,' Margaret retorted. 'Still, I bet Ben enjoyed himself. It was the first time you've taken him abroad, wasn't it? How did he like it?'

'H-he loved it. There were loads of children at the campsite for him to play with. Most of them were French but that didn't seem to stop them from all making friends.' Claire could feel her heart thumping like crazy. She didn't look at Sean but she heard the small thud as he put down his mug. Her palms were suddenly so damp that she had to wipe them down her skirt under cover of the table.

'And who is Ben?'

She jumped as Sean spoke, wondering if only she could hear the edge in his voice. She glanced at Margaret but her friend was busily choosing a biscuit from the tin and seemed oblivious to the tension that suddenly filled the room.

Claire wet her lips but her voice still sounded dry and cracked when it emerged. 'Ben is…is my son.'

Her eyes moved to Sean's face, as though drawn by some magnetic force, but he wasn't looking at her. He was staring down at his tea as if he found the sight of it hypnotic. He suddenly looked up and his eyes seemed to blaze as they met hers.

'I didn't realise that you had a child, Claire. As I said

before, a lot of water has flowed under the bridge, hasn't it?' He stood up abruptly, smiling at Margaret when she looked at him in surprise. 'Thanks for the tea. It was great.'

'You're welcome.' Margaret watched him leave then turned to Claire, making no attempt to hide her curiosity. 'Why do I have the distinct impression that I'm missing something?'

'I don't know what you mean.' Claire got up and took her mug to the sink to wash it. She dried her hands, avoiding Margaret's eyes as she headed for the door. 'I think I'll just go and check the supply cupboard. I noticed one or two items need replacing...'

'Claire Shepherd, you'd try the patience of a saint! Come on, give. You've met our handsome Sean before, haven't you?' Margaret neatly stepped into her path, obviously intending to get an answer one way or the other.

'Oh, all right!' Claire tried to inject a note of exasperation into her voice but she wasn't sure it was wholly convincing. She swallowed hard as she recalled how Sean had looked at her before he'd left the room, almost as though...as though she had let him down!

She blanked out that thought, realising that it was simply the product of her own imagination. Sean might have been surprised to learn she had a child but that was all. Ben's existence would mean little to him and that was how she intended it to remain.

She concentrated instead on what she should tell her friend. She was fond of Margaret but she had told nobody the truth and now it was more imperative than ever that she keep it to herself.

'Sean and I...knew one another some time ago.' She coloured as the hesitation crept in despite her best efforts. She avoided Margaret's eyes as she continued in the same flat tone. 'We worked together in Sheffield. Sean was doing his hospital rotation there before he went out to Africa to work for the United Nations. That's all.'

'All? Hmm, I doubt it was that simple, Claire. But I suppose that's your business and nobody else's.' Margaret smiled but there was still a gleam of curiosity in her eyes. 'Obviously, he didn't know about Ben so I suppose that's why he sounded so shocked just now.'

'I expect so.' Claire looked down at her hands, feeling the hot sting of tears behind her eyelids. 'Sean had left for Africa before Ben was born,' she explained truthfully.

'But he must have known Ben's father, surely? You met him when you worked in Sheffield, didn't you?' Margaret probed. 'I'm surprised you didn't mention him, especially in view of the circumstances. I suppose you didn't quite know how to go about telling Sean he was dead in case he was upset?'

'I…I'm not sure if Sean knew him. Sean might have left to go overseas by the time we…we met.' She saw Margaret open her mouth and suddenly knew that she couldn't take any more questions, no matter how well meaning they were. She stepped around her and hurried from the room, her heart hammering inside her. Had she managed to allay Margaret's suspicions? She wasn't sure.

Panic swirled inside her as she quickly made her way to the office. She closed the door then went to the window and made herself take several deep breaths to contain the fear she felt, but it hovered over her like a huge, dark cloud.

She had told everyone the same story over the years, that Ben's father had died before Ben was born. Even though it had made her feel guilty when people had expressed their sympathy, it had seemed the best way to prevent any awkward questions. Not once in all this time had she told anyone the real truth.

Wasn't that what a court of law demanded? she thought despairingly. The truth, the whole truth and nothing but the truth, before judgement was passed? But how would Sean judge her if she told him the truth? How would he react? What sentence would *he* demand?

She stared towards the hills as the fear grew to overwhelming proportions. How would *any* man feel to suddenly learn he had a seven-year-old son he had never heard about?

'That seems to have sorted things out. The patient should feel a lot more comfortable now.'

Brian Haversham glanced at his watch without bothering to ask Helen Morris how she felt. The drugs Sean had prescribed had worked extremely well to correct her erratic heartbeat. Claire knew that Brian was impatient to get back to the operating theatre but she couldn't help thinking that his bedside manner left a lot to be desired!

'Right, Sister. I want the patient admitted overnight for observation. Ring through to the ward manager and tell him to find her a bed.'

'Yes, sir.' Claire gave Mrs Morris an encouraging smile and mouthed, 'I'll be back in a minute.' Then she escorted the senior registrar from the room. Brian was a stickler for formality, making a fuss if he wasn't afforded the courtesies due to him. It was always so busy in A and E that it annoyed Claire that so much time should be wasted, but she had learned to do what was expected of her. Brian wasn't a good man to cross.

She saw him to the lift then hesitated, wondering if she should risk reminding him about the herbal capsules and their possible link to Mrs Morris's illness. There had been nothing back from the lab as yet, and her own attempts to contact the herbalist had failed as he was away at a conference that day. They had no proof that the capsules were to blame in any way, of course, and it did seem unlikely. However, it didn't seem right that she should avoid mentioning it just because Brian might be impatient about the delay.

'Did Dr Fitzgerald mention that we are checking the herbal medication Mrs Morris has been taking, sir?'

'Yes. Why?' His tone was so blunt that it bordered on rudeness. He didn't have a high opinion of the nursing staff and made no bones about it. It annoyed Claire because she knew that in her own field she was as highly qualified as he was. However, she was also aware that there was a more personal reason for his animosity towards her.

Brian Haversham had asked her out on a date not long after she'd arrived at Dalverston General. It had happened at the Christmas party, which Claire had been persuaded to attend. He had made a pest of himself all night long, refusing to accept that she didn't want to dance with him time after time.

He'd had a little too much to drink and she had attributed his persistence to that. However, he had turned nasty when she had politely refused his offer to take her home. Claire had cut short the threatened scene by walking out of the party, but she knew that Brian still bore her a grudge, which was why she was always extremely circumspect when dealing with him.

'I wondered if you were going to follow it up, sir,' she enquired with a chilly politeness which obviously wasn't lost on him.

He gave her a thin smile, his pale blue eyes full of

dislike. 'I cannot see that there is reason to suspect those capsules have caused the problem, Sister. Frankly, I think Fitzgerald is wasting the lab's time by asking for a report on them. Evening primrose oil, indeed!'

Brian shook his head and sighed. 'God knows why the management saw fit to take him on. They must be desperate, that's all I can say.'

'Dr Fitzgerald is a highly skilled doctor!' Claire retorted sharply. 'Added to that, he has a real rapport with the patients. There are a lot of doctors who could learn a lesson or two from him.'

'I see Dr Fitzgerald has won you over, Sister. However, I shall reserve judgement until I see how he fares. Good day.'

Brian's expression was thunderous as stepped into the lift. Claire sighed. She had a feeling that she had antagonised him even more by jumping to Sean's defence like that. It hadn't been a wise move in view of the fact that he could make things very unpleasant for her if he chose to. She was coming to the end of her stint in A and E and had been hoping to be transferred to one of the surgical wards. She might have scuppered her chances from the look of it!

'Sister, can you take a look at a patient for me, please?' Janet Whately, one of the newest recruits to A and E, called to her, and Claire dragged her mind back to her work.

'What is it, Janet? Problems?' she asked as she went over to the girl.

'I'm not sure. Can you just take a look?' Janet pushed back the floral curtain and led the way into the cubicle. 'This is Mr Simms. He was planing some wood this morning and managed to get sawdust in his left eye. The triage nurse told me to irrigate it with saline solution, which I've done. But I'm not sure if there isn't something left in there.'

'I see.' Claire smiled at the elderly man who was holding a lint pad to his streaming eye. 'Hello, Mr Simms. Whoever said that DIY is a nice safe hobby never worked in an accident unit. You wouldn't believe the number of people we get in here with DIY injuries!'

'Oh, I'd believe it, Sister. Been here a time or two myself over the years.' He managed a smile but Claire could tell that he was in some discomfort. She drew a chair over and sat down so that she was on a level with him, then carefully separated his upper and lower eyelids.

'Has Dr Fitzgerald seen this patient?' Claire asked as she examined the man's eye for any visible sign of a foreign body.

'No. He was busy with another patient, that old lady who'd broken her ankle. Louise told me to irrigate the eye then see how Mr Simms felt.'

Claire nodded. It was normal procedure for the triage nurse to prioritise treatment when A and E was busy, as it had been that morning. The most urgent cases were dealt with first, those of a less serious nature being seen on a rota basis. Something like Mr Simms's injury, whilst uncomfortable for the patient, wasn't a life-and-death situation. However, Claire felt that Sean should take a look at it just to be on the safe side.

'Can you ask Dr Fitzgerald to come in here, Janet, please? I think we should check that there is nothing left in this eye.'

'Yes, Sister.'

The young nurse hurried away as Claire went to fetch the ophthalmoscope. She had it set up and the patient seated in a chair by the time Sean appeared.

'I believe you're worried that there might still be something in Mr Simms's eye, Sister?' Sean queried as he sat down on the chair she had placed in front of the machine.

Claire stilled the flutter her heart gave as he glanced at her and their eyes locked. She kept her tone as neutral as she could make it, but she could hear the quaver in her voice even if Sean couldn't. 'That's right, Dr Fitzgerald. Nurse Whately has irrigated the eye but Mr Simms is still experiencing a lot of discomfort.'

Sean nodded, his expression betraying little as he turned to the patient. 'Well, let's just take a look and see what's in there, shall we? If you could just dim the...' He smiled as Claire turned the cubicle lights to a lower setting so that they wouldn't overpower the ophthalmoscope's light source. 'Mmm, seems you read my mind, Claire.'

The flutter she had felt before was nothing compared to the surge her heart gave as Sean called her by her name in that smoky voice. She bit her lip, using the small, sharp pain it caused to hold onto her control.

It meant nothing, she told herself sternly, nothing at all! Sean was treating her as he would have treated any other colleague...

'Ah, now I see what it is.'

She started as she heard the exclamation he gave. She glanced at him, glad of the muted lighting which hid her heightened colour as he looked round.

'You...you've found something?' she enquired huskily, then wished she had made a better job of disguising her feelings as she saw the way his brows drew together as though something about her tone had troubled him.

'Yes. There's a tiny splinter in the cornea, fortunately just to one side of the pupil. No wonder it's so painful.

I should be able to get it out easily enough but the patient will need a local anaesthetic.' Sean's tone betrayed little but Claire was aware that he was watching her intently.

'Of course. What would you like me to get for you, Doctor?' She forced herself to concentrate as Sean told her what he needed. She repeated his instructions then hurried from the cubicle, glad of the excuse to get away.

She set about collecting what was needed and went back, but found herself hesitating as fear suddenly rose inside her again.

This wasn't going to work! Having Sean here was going to be impossible to deal with on a daily basis. Yet what was the alternative? To give up the life she'd made here for herself and Ben?

She took a deep breath, willing the panic to subside. It was unthinkable to disrupt their lives like that, and pointless in the circumstances. Sean would be here only a few months and then he would move on. Her life would return to normal then.

She pushed back the curtain and felt her heart lurch painfully as her eyes came to rest on the back of Sean's head. Suddenly, she knew that her life would never be the same now that he had come back into it, albeit fleetingly. Losing him once had been bad enough, but losing him a second time would be even more painful. It was only the thought of Ben and how much more she stood to lose which stiffened her resolve.

For all their sakes, but most of all for Ben's sake, Sean must never find out that he had a son!

CHAPTER THREE

'SEE you tomorrow, Margaret. Let's hope it isn't as busy then!'

'Fat chance of that!' Margaret grimaced as she poked her head round her locker door. 'When isn't this place like a madhouse?'

Claire laughed at the wry comment. She left the staff-room, aware that every bit of her was aching. It had been like a baptism of fire, coming back from holiday to a day like this, but she knew that it wasn't just the pressure of keeping on top of the job which had left her feeling so drained. It was the stress of working in such close proximity to Sean which had done most of the damage. If her body had been put through the mill then her emotions had been put through the wringer!

Claire hurried out of the door, anxious to put a little distance between herself and the possibility of bumping into Sean again that day. He had been dealing with a patient when she'd been relieved by the night staff so she'd been spared having to speak to him before she'd left. Now she hurried to the car park and unlocked the door of her old Vauxhall Nova with a sigh of relief. What she needed were a few Sean-free hours to set her back on track!

She started to reverse out of the parking space then groaned as the engine cut out. Turning the key again, she endeavoured to restart it, but the small car was having none of it. There was a miserable whine then nothing after that…

'Having trouble?'

Claire counted to ten before she wound down the window, but even that didn't steady her wildly fluttering pulse as she found Sean crouched down beside the car so that his face was level with hers. His eyes were the deepest, most glorious blue she had ever seen, so that for a crazy moment she had the feeling that she was in danger of drowning in them…

'Claire?' The warm amusement in his voice brought her back to the present with a rush. Claire felt heat sweep through her as she jerked her gaze away from Sean's laughing blue eyes, not allowing herself to wonder what had amused him because she had a feeling that she wouldn't like the answer!

'It's OK. I…I can manage. Thank you,' she said stiffly as she tried the ignition once more, pressing her foot down so hard on the accelerator in her eagerness to make the car start that the smell of petrol wafted around them in a cloud.

'You'll flood the engine if you keep on like that. Here, let me have a go.' Sean was already reaching for the doorhandle when she forestalled him.

'No! I can do it!' Her tone was far sharper than she'd intended, and she saw his brows draw together. There was an edge to his voice all of a sudden which completely erased the friendliness she'd heard in it moments before.

'I'm sure you can. However, there's no need to bite my head off, Claire. I was just offering to help, that's all.'

His face was set as he walked over to his own car. He started the engine then drove off without a glance in her direction. Claire felt hot tears sting her eyes and blinked hard to stop them from falling, but she couldn't dislodge the lump of misery that was stuck in her throat. It shouldn't matter that she had offended Sean by her abrupt refusal of his help, but it did.

She spent the next ten minutes trying, unsuccessfully, to get the car to start before finally giving up. Locking the door, she headed out of the car park and made her way towards the nearest bus stop. However, she had gone no more than a few hundred yards when a car drew up alongside her. Sean leaned across the passenger seat and opened the door.

'Get in, Claire. I'll give you a lift.'

'There's no need...' she began.

He swore softly, his eyes full of impatience as they blazed at her. 'For heaven's sake, woman! Are you trying to make this situation even more difficult than it is?'

'I wasn't... I mean, I'm not...' She looked despairingly along the road then sighed as she realised that he was right. If it had been any other of her workmates she would have gratefully accepted the offer without a second thought. But, then, none of the people she worked with meant as much to her as Sean had once done.

'I'm sorry. It's just all so strange, you coming back like this when I never expected it,' she admitted softly, knowing that she owed him an apology.

'I know.' His tone gentled all of a sudden. 'Do you think it isn't difficult for me, too, Claire?'

She shrugged but the quiet confession tugged at her heartstrings. 'I don't know. You tell me.'

'I will...if you'll get in.' He suddenly grinned, his face lighting up with laughter as he looked pointedly across the road. 'I'll even say please if you want. I don't fancy getting locked up in a cell for kerb-crawling on my first day in this town!'

Claire followed his gaze and gasped as she spotted the

police car parked on the other side of the road. It was obvious that the police officers were watching what was going on *and* putting their own interpretation on it from the looks on their faces! It helped her make up her mind.

She slid into the seat, slamming the door as Sean pulled smoothly out into the traffic. He shot her a glance, his face still holding that same warm amusement which did all sorts of dangerous things to her blood pressure.

'Thank you. I think you just saved my reputation and maybe even my job. I don't imagine the hospital authorities would look too kindly on a new locum being hauled in by the police!' he teased.

'I...I'm sure it wouldn't have come to that,' she replied stiltedly, wishing she could respond more naturally to the laughing remark. Sean was doing his best to put her at ease but she just couldn't seem to follow his lead.

She took a deep breath, trying to ignore the thunderous pounding of her heart, but it was hard to pretend she didn't hear it in the close confines of the car. Could Sean hear it, too? she wondered. She had no idea but the thought that he might start wondering about the way she was behaving made her more nervous than ever so that she actually jumped when his arm brushed hers as he changed gear.

She shot him a glance from wary brown eyes and saw the wry smile he gave her in return. 'Relax, Claire. I'm just giving you a lift home, that's all. There's no need to look so uptight. Surely it's the least an old friend can do?'

He was simply reiterating his earlier statement—that he wanted them to be friends—yet she found herself wondering if he found it as difficult as she did to separate his feelings into nice tidy compartments. What she felt for Sean was bound up by so many emotions apart from friendship that it was hard to sort one out from another and yet she had to try, otherwise the next few months were going to be a nightmare.

'Thank you,' she said quietly. 'I...I appreciate it.'

'You're welcome.' He inclined his head gravely but there was a hint of curiosity in the look he gave her. 'So, how long have you lived in this part of the world, then?'

'Just over a year now,' she replied carefully, feeling her heart skip a beat. It was natural that Sean should ask questions about what had happened to her over the past eight years, but it didn't make things any easier. Knowing that she must be on her guard was even more of a strain so that she wished with her whole heart that she could think of an excuse to get out of the car. It was only the thought that it might arouse his suspicions that stopped her.

'And you like it here? You don't miss the city at all?' Sean continued smoothly.

'Not really.' Claire glanced at him but there was nothing on his face other than that same polite interest so she let herself relax a little. 'I've always loved this area and coming here hasn't changed my views one bit.'

'It must have been a big change for you, though. You must have had to adapt your whole way of life, I imagine?'

'Yes and no.' Claire smiled as she saw him frown at the ambiguity of her answer. 'I know I'd always lived in a city before but I never led a hectic social life. In fact, I've made far more friends since I came here. Oh, there are odd things I miss, like trips to the theatre or an exhibition, but I went so rarely that it hasn't been a problem. I can honestly say that moving here was the best thing I could have done, for Ben as well as myself, because he's been so much better.'

Too late she realized what she had done by mentioning her son. She stared out of the window, wondering if she imagined the strain she heard in Sean's voice.

'What do you mean—better? Is there something wrong with him?'

'He…he suffers from asthma. However, since we moved out of the city the number of attacks he's had have dropped dramatically,' she explained quietly.

'I see. Obviously, living here has done him good, then. And you, too, I imagine. There's nothing more stressful than watching a child suffer unnecessarily.'

Sean's tone gave little away yet she sensed there was a deeper meaning to the quietly spoken words. She looked at him and her heart started aching at the sadness she saw on his face. 'Are you thinking about the children you treated in Africa?' she asked softly.

He smiled sadly, his blue eyes playing over her face for a moment before he concentrated on the traffic again. 'Yes. Although for far too many there was no treatment we could give them. By the time they got to the hospital they were too ill to save. The best we could do was to make them comfortable.'

'It…it must have been awful. How did you cope?'

'You just do.' His hands tightened on the steering-wheel, belying the apparent calmness of the statement. 'Once you're put in a situation like that the only thing you can do is cope with it. You and the rest of the medical team are the only hope those people have.'

'Were you in Africa all the time? Or did you go anywhere else? You wanted to go to Australia at one time, didn't you?'

'You remember that?' There was a searching quality

to the look he gave her as they drew up at a junction. Claire felt herself colour and looked away, but she was afraid she hadn't been quick enough. If Sean had any idea how much she remembered...!

She blanked out the thought, concentrating instead on what was happening now rather than what had gone on in the past. It would serve no purpose to rake it all up again, it would just cause untold damage. How would Ben feel if he discovered that his father was alive and that she had lied to him all this time?

Claire felt the panic rise to the surface again as she thought about how hurt Ben would be and how confused. It was hard to keep any trace of it out of her voice. 'Of course I remember.' She gave a light laugh, praying it would convince him that she was telling the truth. 'Let's face it, Sean, you told me about your plans often enough!'

'Yes, I did, didn't I?' He drew out of the junction and picked up speed as they cleared the worst of the traffic. The hospital was one of the newest in the region and had been built on the site of the old Victorian hospital which had served the bustling north Lancashire town for many years. Various shops and offices had sprung up around it over the years, making the whole area a nightmare to get into and out of during rush hour.

There had been talk of expanding the hospital in the future, which could only exacerbate the traffic problems, but apart from an upgrading of the maternity unit nothing else had happened so far.

'We spent hours talking about Africa and Australia, didn't we, Claire? About all the things we wanted to see and do, how we wanted to change people's lives for the better.' He gave a harsh laugh which made her flinch. 'Pipe dreams!'

'What do you mean? You must have made a difference to a lot of people's lives, Sean,' she said in confusion.

'I'd like to think so, but I'm not conceited enough to believe that my contribution was anything more than a drop in the ocean. However, I wasn't referring to what I did out in Africa or even what I learned in Australia because, yes, I did make it there as well. I spent a couple of years in Sydney, working in one of their top hospitals. I was talking about the dreams *we* had, you and me, how we would spend our lives together. All that went up in smoke, didn't it, Claire? It was one thing to talk about it and another to face the reality of what we were planning.'

He shrugged as he looked at her again. 'Was that why you decided against going with me in the end? Because you couldn't face the thought of the conditions you would meet?'

'Yes,' Claire whispered. She avoided his eyes as she strove to convince him but the lie almost choked her. 'I couldn't face the thought of the heat, the lack of facilities…all those things.'

'You wanted more from life than a lot of dirt and dust and patients who couldn't be saved?' Sean laughed bitterly. 'And who could blame you? It just shows how arrogant I was to believe you wanted what I did because it would mean us being together. At the end of the day, Claire, you wanted a lot more than I was offering, didn't you?'

Claire was so choked by emotion that she couldn't speak and Sean put his own interpretation on her silence. 'I thought so. At least you're honest enough not to deny it. Why should you? It appears you found what you wanted in the end. Tell me about Ben's father, Claire.

You haven't mentioned him yet. What does he do? Is he in the medical profession as well? Or were you wise enough to chose someone outside our field?'

He gave another short laugh. 'I've just realised that I don't even know the guy's name!'

The panic which had been floating just beneath the surface seemed to double in intensity so that Claire wondered wildly if she was going to be sick.

'Claire? Are you OK?' Sean drew the car into the kerb as he saw her stricken face. His eyes were full of concern as he caught hold of her cold hands. 'What is it? Don't you feel well?'

She jerked her hands away, terrified that his touch would be the catalyst to set loose everything she was struggling to contain. 'I'm fine. I…I'm just a bit tired, that's all. Probably with coming back from holiday last night and going straight into work this morning.'

Sean's eyes darkened with sudden comprehension. 'Possibly. However, I imagine this situation is more to blame.' He glanced at her hands, which were tightly clasped in her lap, and sighed wearily. 'I apologise, Claire. I never intended to upset you. It never does any good, raking over the past, does it? You have my word that from now on I won't mention it again. Now, if you'd just tell me where you want to be dropped off…'

She looked around, realising with a start where they were. 'Here will do fine,' she replied numbly, reaching for the doorhandle. 'I only live a short walk from here so there's no point in taking you any further out of your way.'

She opened the door and got out of the car, then paused, unable to bring herself to walk away without saying something…

She took a deep breath, fighting an almost overwhelming urge to explain the *real* reason she'd refused to go with him all those years ago. It would serve no purpose now yet the desire to tell Sean the truth was so great that her voice quavered with the effort it cost her not to say anything.

'Thank you for the lift, Sean. I'll see you tomorrow, I expect.'

He inclined his head, although he didn't say anything. Claire watched him drive away then quickly made her way home to the small terraced house where she lived. She took a deep breath before slipping her key into the lock, wanting to be sure there was no trace of what she was feeling on her face when she saw Ben. But she could feel the agony of indecision throbbing inside her like a wound which had turned septic.

Had she been right to leave Sean in ignorance all this time? Had she been right to deny Ben a father who would have loved him? Suddenly she wasn't sure any more. Even the old arguments which had led up to her decision didn't seem as strong as they had been.

She ran through them again, wanting to convince herself that she had been right to do what she had. She hadn't wanted Sean to feel that he'd had to give up all his dreams. He had set his heart on going overseas to work but she had known that he would have refused to go if he'd found out about the baby. She hadn't wanted to run the risk that at some point he would come to resent his plans being ruined and blame her or, worse still, Ben, for ruining them.

Hadn't her own father once flung that accusation at her—that he had only married her mother because she'd been expecting Claire? Although Claire had been just a child at the time, the remark had made a huge impact on her. The thought that her child might one day be blamed, as she had been, for something he'd had no control over had terrified her. There had been no option but to let Sean go overseas ignorant of the fact that she'd been expecting his baby.

Claire stood on the step, remembering why she had decided not to tell Sean that she was pregnant. Her reasons were as valid now as they had been then, yet it didn't comfort her to realise that. She still felt an overwhelming sense of guilt and regret, even though she knew how futile it was.

Ben must have heard her opening the door because he came racing out of the kitchen to meet her, the moustache of milk on his upper lip a testament to what he had been doing.

'Hi, Mum, you're late. Where have you been?' he demanded, taking her bag to hang it on the hook. It was a ritual they'd had since Ben was tiny—she would give him her bag when she got home from work and he would hang it up for her, although until a few months ago she had needed to lift him up to reach the peg.

Now she felt a wave of tenderness swamp her as she realised how tall Ben had grown, felt the pang which followed it as he turned and grinned at her. He had her colouring, the same dark red hair with a tendency to curl and skin that burned far too easily in the sun, but his eyes were Sean's, sapphire blue and ringed with thick black lashes...

'Mum?'

Claire jumped, realising that Ben was looking puzzled because she hadn't answered his question. 'Oh, the car wouldn't start. I had to leave it in the car park at work. That's why I'm late.'

'Oh, no! I wanted to go to Tim's tonight, too. Still,

maybe he can get his mum to bring him over here instead. Is that OK, Mum?'

Ben brightened up as she nodded. He raced back into the kitchen to phone his friend and tell him about the change of plans. Claire took off her coat and followed him, exchanging a few words with Mrs Mitchell, the elderly widow from next door who looked after Ben when he got home from school.

After Mrs Mitchell had gone, Claire opened the fridge, realising as she saw the empty shelves that she would have to go shopping soon. 'Not much of a choice, I'm afraid. How about scrambled eggs for tea?'

'Great. And sausages? I think there's some in the freezer. I'll have a look.' Ben rushed to the freezer as he finished his phone call and found the packet of sausages. He gave them to Claire then picked up his glass of milk. 'How did you get home, Mum? Did you catch the bus?'

'No.' She arranged a row of sausages across the grill pan. 'I got a lift back.'

'Who from?' Ben took his empty glass to the sink and turned on the tap. Claire took a deep breath but suddenly the sausages were obscured by a mist of tears.

'Nobody you know,' she replied softly.

'RTA arriving ten minutes,' Claire called over her shoulder. She carried on making notes on the pad as she listened to the paramedic's voice coming over the radio. 'Three adults. Crush injuries. One child. Possible fractured skull. Right, got that.'

'Is the trauma unit free yet?' Sean had come up behind her and was reading over her shoulder. Claire carefully wiped all expression from her face as she turned, wishing she could erase the quiver which ran through her body as well—but that was impossible.

Sean had stayed true to his promise ever since they had come on duty that morning. He had kept any conversations strictly confined to matters concerning their patients. It had helped, but it didn't prevent the rush of awareness she felt right then as she realised how close he was standing to her.

She could smell the scent of his skin, that clean aroma of antiseptic soap and another perfume which was intrinsically his, and her mind spun…

She fought free of the memories as she replied to his question. 'Dr Hill has just transferred the young man who lost his hand in the threshing machine to the operating theatre. Fortunately, somebody had the presence of mind to pack the hand in ice and send it along in the ambulance so there's a chance it can be sewn back on. The domestics are cleaning up in there at the moment, but they won't be long.'

She paused thoughtfully. 'We could move the angina case, if you think it's safe to do so, and put him in the side room. Mrs Dennis, the lady with the broken hip, is in there at the moment, but she'll be going up to Theatre as soon as they can take her, which shouldn't be long now. Anyway, there's room for two beds at a squeeze.'

'I'm not sure.' Sean glanced at his watch and frowned. 'How long have we got before the ambulance gets here?'

'Ten minutes, maybe a little more at this time of the morning. The traffic will still be heavy so they might have a job getting through it.'

'Then I'll just take another look at Mr Finch. I don't want to run the risk of moving him until I'm sure he's stable.'

Sean headed swiftly in the direction of the trauma

unit. Claire followed, knowing that whatever he decided it would be up to her to make the arrangements. The reception area was a sea of expectant faces as she passed through it. She could hear a man giving one of the receptionists hell about the length of time he'd had to wait, but she took no notice until he deliberately stepped into her path.

'So, there are some nurses in this place! I was beginning to think you were all on your teabreaks. Perhaps you could spare the time to take a look at my hand, Nurse, if it isn't too much trouble, of course?'

Claire stared him straight in the eye. Experience had taught her that there was just one way to handle a patient like this, and that was by not losing her temper. 'I'm afraid we have been exceptionally busy this morning, sir. I apologise for the delay but unfortunately there's little we can do about it. We're expecting an emergency to arrive in the next few minutes so we need to keep everything clear while we deal with that.'

She went to move on but the man obviously didn't intend to let her get away that easily. She saw Sean stop and glance round just as the man stepped in front of her again.

'Do you know who I am, Nurse?' he enquired menacingly.

Claire fixed a smile to her lips. 'I'm afraid not. However, it makes little difference who you are, sir. Emergencies must and do take priority in this department.' She glanced at his hand. The cut across his palm had stopped bleeding, although it might require a couple of stitches. However, it was hardly a life-threatening condition! 'A nurse will see to your hand just as soon as we have one free. Now, if you'll excuse me...'

'Don't think you're going to get away with this!' He

grabbed hold of her arm, his fingers closing bruisingly around it so that involuntarily Claire winced. 'I know a lot of important people in this hospital—'

'Then you should know how to behave.' Sean's voice was low yet the note it held made the man swing around. Sean gave him a thin smile before his eyes dropped pointedly to his hand, which was still clamped around Claire's arm.

'I suggest you let Sister go, sir. It would be a shame to add to your injuries, especially as we are too busy to attend to them at present.'

It was all said in such a silkily smooth voice that Claire blinked, wondering if she had heard it correctly. She took a quick step back as the man abruptly released her, rubbing the top of her arm to restore the circulation.

Sean shot her a look and she felt a shiver run through her as she saw the anger in his eyes, even though she knew it wasn't directed at her.

'Are you all right, Sister? Would you like me to call the police so that you can press charges? Physical assault is an offence.'

Claire shook her head. 'No. There's no need for that. I'm sure this gentleman didn't realise he was hurting me.'

'Sure?' Sean gave her a moment to reconsider then turned to the man, who seemed to be experiencing some difficulty in breathing from the way his mouth kept opening and closing. 'I think an apology is called for, don't you, sir? Especially as Sister Shepherd has taken such a lenient view of you molesting her?'

'Molesting... Why... You... Don't think you're going to get away with this! I intend to take this to the very highest level!' The man turned and stamped his way to the door, the cut on his hand obviously forgotten. He treated them to a venomous look then disappeared. There was a moment's silence then someone started to clap. The applause was quickly picked up by the rest of the patients in the waiting area.

June, the receptionist who had been dealing with him, leaned over the counter. 'I think that says it all! Everyone here was heartily sick of listening to him carrying on about how long he'd had to wait and how he didn't have time to waste because he had more important things to do!'

'Glad to be of service.' Sean grinned. He turned and took a mocking bow, laughing as the waiting patients sent up a small cheer. However, his face sobered abruptly as he led Claire out of Reception. 'Sure you're all right?'

'I'm fine. Honestly. It takes more than an irate patient to rattle me!' she replied lightly, still rather stunned by the speed and determination with which Sean had handled the unpleasant incident.

'Hmm, I wonder what it does take?' The question was barely out before he turned away. He was all business once more as he led the way to the trauma room. 'I'll just check the monitor readings,' he said shortly as he went to the bed, 'then we'll see about moving Mr Finch.'

Claire nodded, although she didn't say anything. She couldn't! She felt too breathless to speak and too disturbed to sort her thoughts into any logical sequence either. She busied herself, tidying the room, instructing the nurse who had been sitting with the patient that everything not in use was to be cleared away.

Quickly and efficiently, she went through the supplies, sending the junior for more saline and sterile dressings, even ordering a second portable X-ray machine to be brought in. She did everything required of her, and did it with her usual efficiency. Only she knew that one part of her mind was still wondering what Sean had meant.

What did he think it would take to disturb her? Did he remember how *he* used to disturb her? Perhaps that was the most disquieting thought of all!

CHAPTER FOUR

'I'M SORRY about this, Mrs Dennis. Normally we wouldn't double patients up in here, but we've an ambulance coming in with four emergency cases so we're a bit stuck for space.'

Claire smiled at the elderly woman as she took her pulse. She noted the reading on the chart then hung it back on the bottom of the bed. 'You seem to be doing fine, anyway. And it won't be long before you go up to Theatre now.'

'Don't you go worrying about me, Sister. I'm nothing but a silly old fool, that's what I am.' The old lady sighed. 'Falling out of bed at my age and putting everyone to all this trouble!'

'It's just one of those things, Mrs Dennis. It happens to a lot of people your age and plenty a lot younger than you, in fact,' Claire added truthfully.

'Don't make no difference. So I'm eighty-six—that don't mean I'm senile, but that's how I feel.' The old lady grimaced. 'I hope this won't mean I'll have to give up me dancing, though. They will be able to mend this here hip, won't they?'

'Dancing?' Claire repeated, wondering if the old lady was joking. However, Mrs Dennis's expression was completely serious.

'Aye. Sequence dancing. We do it twice a week, Tuesdays and Thursdays. I really look forward to it, I can tell you. Mind, there's been that much to do since I moved in that I often wonder why they call it a "rest" home. I hardly have a moment to myself, what with the outings and craft classes they put on for us.'

The old lady's face broke into a smile despite the pain she was in. 'Some of the old folk there call the place God's waiting-room, and happen it is. But I mean to enjoy every moment I have there! So tell that doctor I want a good job done on my hip, will you, Sister? I don't intend to end my days as a wallflower!'

'I shall pass the message on, Mrs Dennis!' Claire was still laughing as she left the room. She stopped to have a word with the pleasant-faced care assistant who had accompanied the old lady to the hospital.

'Mrs Dennis will be going up to Theatre shortly. They're going to give her the pre-med down here as there's a bit of a backlog upstairs. You did say that she hadn't had anything to eat since last night?'

'That's right. All the residents have supper around eight before we start getting them off to their beds.' The woman sighed. 'I feel so guilty. The poor dear must have been lying on the floor for a couple of hours before we found her. We check on all the residents throughout the night but we try not to disturb them too much. And Mrs Dennis is remarkably fit for her age, or has been up till now.'

'There's no reason why she won't be up and about again,' Claire said comfortingly. 'It will take a bit of time, but with care and the right physiotherapy she should be on her feet, even back to her dancing classes, before too long. You go and have a word with her and then get off. She'll be fine with us.'

Claire hurried on her way, quietly opening the door to the trauma unit. Sean was standing beside the bed, keenly watching the monitor as it flickered out its information. He looked up as Claire approached and his gaze was thoughtful.

'Mr Finch seems to be a bit more stable now. From what I can gather, he's had angina for some time. It was just unfortunate that he left his hotel this morning without remembering to take his tablets with him.'

'What does he take?' Claire asked. 'Glyceryl trinitrate?'

'Mmm. It's remarkably effective in easing the pain of an attack, as you know, but the effects wear off after about twenty or thirty minutes. I have a feeling from what the driver told me when he brought Mr Finch in that the attacks have been getting more frequent recently, too.'

Claire moved away from the bed, frowning as she considered what Sean had said. 'If that's the case, why hasn't he been back to see his own doctor?'

'I've no idea.' Sean came to join her. His expression also was puzzled as he looked at the middle-aged man who now had his eyes closed. 'To be frank, Mr Finch has been less than co-operative. Getting information out of him has been like drawing teeth. He seems more annoyed than grateful that his chauffeur had the sense to bring him straight here. I've had the devil's own job keeping him quiet while we monitor what's going on, and I'm not too happy with the results either.'

'Why not? Surely, if the patient is receiving treatment then his doctor will be checking for signs of deterioration in his condition?' Claire queried.

'You'd think so.' Sean sounded sceptical. 'But from what I can gather, it appears that Mr Finch has missed his last few appointments. In my opinion, surgery is his best option now. It's obvious he can't keep on like this, with the attacks becoming ever more frequent and violent.'

'A bypass, you mean?' Claire suggested.

'I think it's heading that way—' Sean broke off as the man suddenly opened his eyes and tried to sit up. He hurried to the bed, pressing him gently back again. 'Just take it easy, Mr Finch. You're not going anywhere yet awhile. We need to make sure that things have settled down first.'

'Nonsense! I've had these attacks dozens of times and this one was no worse than the others. I have a meeting I need to attend. I can't waste time, lying around here!' the man replied hotly.

Sean's brows rose as he glanced at Claire. 'Everyone is in such a rush this morning, aren't they, Sister?'

Claire bit back a smile. First that man in Reception couldn't wait to be seen and now Mr Finch couldn't wait to leave!

Her smile faded abruptly as she realised how easily she had understood what Sean had meant. But it had always been the same, their thoughts had always been so in tune...

She cut short that thought, concentrating instead on what was happening as Sean quietly informed their reluctant patient that he was to be moved to a side room. Mr Finch accepted the refusal to let him leave with ill grace and only after he'd told Sean that he wanted to see his chauffeur as soon as he'd been settled.

Claire set about making the transfer as stress-free as possible. They would need to use all the monitoring equipment in the trauma unit for the incoming accident victims, but there were two sets in the side room so that wasn't a problem.

She and Margaret swiftly unhooked the electrodes

from Mr Finch's chest and arms then set about moving the bed next door rather than disturb him. Sean and one of the porters also lent a hand, although Sean had to leave before they had finished setting everything up.

'There's the ambulance. I'll go and meet it,' he hurriedly informed Claire as they heard the sirens.

'Margaret may as well go with you. I'll finish up in here,' Claire offered. 'I'll be there as soon as I can.'

'Right.' Sean left the room, with Margaret hurrying after him, while Claire finished attaching the last of the electrodes to the patient. She checked the monitor to make sure everything was working properly then turned to leave the room.

'I need a word with my chauffeur. Don't forget now, Nurse!'

She glanced round, frowning as she saw Mr Finch struggling to sit up again. She went back to the bed and injected a firm note of authority into her voice. 'I haven't forgotten, Mr Finch. But you are to lie still. You aren't doing yourself any good by getting excited like this.'

He gave a grumbling reply, closing his eyes in exasperation. Claire gave him a last considering look. She would have liked to have detailed a nurse to sit with him again but, with the new emergency cases coming in, there simply wasn't enough staff.

'Some don't have the sense they're born with, do they, Sister?'

Claire looked round and smiled as she found Mrs Dennis watching what was going on. She went to the bed and bent down so that only Mrs Dennis could hear what she said. 'Not all our patients are as easy to deal with as you, Mrs Dennis!'

The old lady chuckled. 'I s'pose that's because I've gone past the point of worrying about rushing here and there. At my age you try to make each minute last as long as possible ’cos it might be your last!’

Claire laughed at this bit of homespun wisdom. She hurried to the door, nodding to the nurse who was just coming in with Mrs Dennis’s pre-medication. Not only would the drugs sedate the old lady and ease her pain, they would also cut down the amount of anaesthetic needed to keep her unconscious during the operation on her hip, a vital consideration in a patient of her age.

Leaving the nurse to her job, Claire made her way swiftly to the forecourt in time to see the last of the accident victims being carefully lifted from the second of the two ambulances which had ferried them to the hospital. She felt her heart contract as she saw the small form lying beneath the blankets and realised that it was a boy of about Ben’s age.

The ambulance crew had fitted him with a cervical collar and his face above it was waxen, apart from a huge contusion on the right side of his head. He was deeply unconscious, an oxygen mask over his nose and mouth assisting his breathing. He gave no response when Sean crouched down beside the stretcher and said his name.

‘Simon…can you hear me? Simon?’ Sean shook his head as he stood up. ‘Nothing. Has he come round at all since you picked him up?’

‘No.’ Jenny Partridge, one of the ambulance crew who had attended the call, sighed. ‘He was out for the count when we found him. From what we could tell, he must have hit his head on a stone wall. We fitted a collar then got him straight here, but he’s been unconscious throughout.’

Claire frowned as she followed the trolley inside, holding the clear Perspex swing door open so that the

IV line which was supplying vital fluids to the child wouldn't snag on the way in. 'What was he doing in the road?'

Jenny shrugged. 'We can only assume he was thrown from the car. There were no witnesses so we don't have much idea how the accident happened. But one side of the vehicle had been ripped off when it hit the bridge. I imagine the child was thrown out then.'

'Hmm, I suppose you're right. But it's odd that he wasn't wearing a seat belt when the other passengers were,' Claire observed thoughtfully. However, she had no time to dwell on it as they pushed open the doors to the trauma unit. Three of the beds were already occupied by the adult victims of the crash, and nurses were going through the familiar routine of cutting away clothing so that injuries could be dealt with.

Dr Hill, the consultant on A and E, was trying to assess the damage suffered by a woman in the bed nearest the door. 'Crush injuries to the right side of the chest, three...no, possibly four ribs broken—'

He broke off as the young woman gurgled and started struggling to remove the oxygen mask from her face. 'Right, everyone, we have a pneumothorax. I'll need a chest drain here... Claire?'

'Right away, Doctor.'

Claire moved swiftly across the room and collected the tray containing everything needed to drain the air from the pleural cavity. The young woman's lung had been punctured by a broken rib, allowing air to seep into the space. Not only did it make it difficult for her to breathe, there was also the danger of the heart being compressed as more air collected in the pleural cavity.

By the time she went back, Margaret and one of the junior nurses had manoeuvred the woman into position so that Dr Hill could insert the drain tube through her chest wall.

'There...that's got it!' Dr Hill smiled as bubbles began to appear in the bottle of sterile water into which the tube led, a sure sign that the trapped air was escaping. He watched for a moment but the woman was already breathing more easily now that the pressure had been released.

He nodded in satisfaction. 'Right, apart from those ribs, she doesn't appear to have suffered too much damage. Her right arm is fractured just above the wrist. And there's a possible fracture to the right tibia as well, so we'll take X-rays, if you could set up the machine, Claire.'

'Right away.' Claire swiftly manoeuvred the X-ray machine along its overhead gantry while Margaret covered the patient's abdomen with a lead-lined blanket. Although the woman was conscious she was in no fit state to answer questions coherently and there was no point in taking risks. If it turned out that she was pregnant, exposing the foetus to an X-ray could cause irreversible damage.

The staff moved a safe distance away while the X-ray was taken. Claire quietly instructed one of the nurses to attend to the films while she checked on the rest of the patients. One man was already on his way to surgery. Tom Hartley, the surgical registrar who had been called down to assist, was supervising the transfer himself.

'Ruptured spleen,' he advised Claire succinctly. 'It will be touch and go from the look of it, too.'

Claire nodded, understanding only too well how urgent it was that the spleen be removed as soon as possible. A ruptured spleen bled extensively and the patient could die if the bleeding wasn't stopped quickly.

Although the man had other injuries—a fractured jaw and cheekbone—dealing with this took priority.

The third victim, also a man, seemed to have fared better than his friends. He'd been the driver of the car and, apart from a cut on his chin, he seemed to have escaped with miraculously few injuries. Louise Graham was stitching the gash together, no easy task in view of his agitation.

The man pushed her aside as he leaned forward to speak to Claire. 'How's the kid? He is all right, isn't he? I didn't mean to hit him…!'

He broke off on a sob. Louise pursed her lips, saying nothing, but Claire understood. She, too, had noticed the strong smell of alcohol on the man's breath.

She clamped down on the anger she felt that this carnage might have been avoided if he'd had the sense not to drink and drive. It would be up to the police to ensure he didn't do it again. Now her main concern was the child because it appeared that they had all misread the situation.

'The boy wasn't in the car with you, then?' she asked, her icy tone cutting through the man's noisy sobs.

'No. He…he was crossing the road when I came round the corner…' The driver took a gulping breath. 'I tried to miss him, Nurse. I did!'

Claire hardened her heart, not that it was difficult. She wasn't about to waste sympathy on someone who didn't deserve any. 'Then you have no idea who he is?'

The man shook his head. Claire moved to the end bed where Sean was attending to the boy. His face was very grave as he looked up. 'His skull is fractured. And he has a broken pelvis, possibly some internal damage as well. We need to get him upstairs for a CT scan as soon as possible. If there is fluid building up inside his skull then it will need trephining. We'll need to get a consent form signed a.s.a.p.'

'Could be a problem.' Claire nodded towards the man in the next bed. 'That's the driver of the car, and according to him the boy wasn't with them. He was crossing the road when the car hit him so we don't know who he is.'

'Damn!' Sean turned to Janet, who had been assisting him. 'Get on to the CT unit and warn them we're sending a patient up, please. Tell them it's urgent and that we can't wait.'

Janet hurried away to make the call as Sean bent down to the child again, carefully raising his eyelids to shine a light into them. The left pupil was fixed and didn't respond to the stimulus.

'We can't afford to waste time with this, Claire,' he said shortly. 'The longer we wait the more damage will be done. See if you can get the police to find out who the kid is...' He paused. 'Wait a moment. The ambulance crew called him Simon—how did they know his name? Maybe that's a lead.'

'I'll check it out.' Claire quickly left the room. She hurried along the corridor, pausing momentarily as she remembered that she hadn't given Mr Finch's chauffeur the message before she carried on. It would have to wait. She had more pressing matters to attend to at the moment.

She tracked down the ambulance crews by means of their radios. Both vehicles were in the bay, being cleaned, before they went out again. Claire got Jenny on the line and asked her how she had known the child's name was Simon.

'From his schoolbag. His name is written inside the flap. Why?' Jenny queried, obviously puzzled.

Claire quickly filled her in, then cut short the conversation when it became obvious that Jenny couldn't tell her anything more. She went back to the trauma unit and found the boy's belongings in a plastic bag beside the bed.

The schoolbag was right at the bottom, under his clothing. Claire held up a bloodstained green jumper and realised with a pang that it was the uniform of the school Ben attended. The boy might be in Ben's class for all she knew. It made her feel even worse about what had happened and more determined than ever to find out who he was.

She opened the bag and found his name neatly printed inside the flap, as Jenny had said—Simon Berry.

Taking the bag with her, Claire went to find the police officers who had accompanied the ambulance to the hospital and were waiting to speak to the driver of the car. She quickly outlined the problem, glad when one of them immediately promised to contact the school to find out the boy's address.

Claire left him to it, wondering sadly how Simon's parents were going to feel when they heard about their son…

'Claire, quick!'

She swung round as she heard the anxious cry. She ran as fast as she could to the side room. Mike Kennedy, the male nurse who worked their shift, had gone back inside. When Claire pushed open the door she could see him bent over the bed, performing chest compressions on Mr Finch.

'What happened? Why didn't the alarm go off?' she demanded, hurrying to the bed and reaching for the alarm button to summon assistance.

'It wasn't connected. In fact, several of the electrodes

weren't in place and the plug wasn't in the socket properly.' Mike was panting as he carried on with the compressions.

Claire shot a disbelieving look at the electrocardiograph. She *knew* she'd checked that everything had been set up correctly before she'd left the room, so what had happened?

There was no time to dwell on it, however. Claire took over the task of ventilating the patient, barely glancing up as Sean came into the room.

'What's happened here?' he demanded. 'Why didn't the alarm go off?'

Mike shrugged. 'Some of the electrodes weren't in place. God knows why. I only looked in because there's a man in Reception wanting to know if he should wait. This guy's chauffeur, I believe.'

'I see.' Sean didn't say anything more but his voice held a note that made Claire go cold. Did he think that she'd made a mistake and not set up the equipment properly? She was sure she had done it correctly yet the nagging worry that maybe she was to blame in some way wasn't easy to ignore.

'Right. We'll have to defibrillate. Stand clear.'

Claire and Mike stepped back as Sean positioned the defibrillation paddles on the patient's chest, one just below the right clavicle, the other over the cardiac apex. The electric shock that passed into the patient's body would hopefully restart his heart.

Mike checked for a pulse and shook his head. 'Nothing.'

'Right, let's give it another go. Clear!' Sean repeated the procedure three more times, but the response was negative each time. Some forty minutes later, he sighed as he looked at Claire and Mike. 'I think we've done all we can. Agreed?'

Claire nodded, feeling, as she always did in a situation such as this, a deep sense of regret that their efforts had been in vain. She looked at Sean. 'Will you tell Mr Finch's chauffeur what's happened? Or shall I do it? We'll need to get in touch with his family.'

'I'll do it.' Sean turned to Mike. 'Can you take him to the relatives' room, Mike? I'll be there in a moment.'

Mike nodded, although Claire noticed the look he cast her on his way out of the room. She took a deep breath, realising what was behind it. 'I'm sure that I set everything up correctly, Sean. I know I was in a rush—we all were—but I checked the machine was working properly before I left.'

'I'm sure you did. Look, Claire, I'm in no doubt that you did everything exactly as it should have been done.' He shrugged. 'If the alarm had gone off then it would have given us a bit more time, but I doubt it would have affected the outcome. At the end of the day, the patient himself was to blame for ignoring the warning signs.'

'Maybe.' Claire looked shakily towards the bed. 'But that doesn't stop me wondering—'

'Stop it!' There was impatience in Sean's voice as he propelled her from the room. He swung her round to face him, his hands gripping her shoulders as he bent to look straight into her eyes. 'We do the best we can, Claire, but we aren't God! You're a first-rate nurse and neither I nor anyone else who works with you are in any doubt that you did everything you should have done.'

His voice suddenly deepened and the hands which had been gripping her gentled. 'So don't go blaming yourself for something you couldn't have changed.'

Claire just managed to contain the shiver that ran

through her. She wasn't sure if Sean was aware that his thumbs were painting lazy circles on her flesh through the thin cotton of her uniform dress, but she was! She could feel the tingles those soft caresses were sending through her body, feel how they fanned out from those two small points of contact like rays from the sun, so that it felt as though she were being suffused with heat.

Her eyes lifted to Sean's, the giddy awareness of what she was feeling making her mind run off at a tangent. What would it be like to have Sean make love to her again? Would it be as wonderful as it used to be? Would it be better? Would her body remember his and know instinctively how to respond? Or would it be like going back to the beginning and learning all over again…?

'One thing I have learned, Claire, is that it's pointless to have regrets. We do what we have to and that's the end of it. Wishing we'd done things differently doesn't change a damn thing!'

The sudden bitterness in his voice broke the spell. Claire took a jolting breath as she stepped away from him, even though her body ached at the loss of contact. For a moment she stared into his deep blue eyes before she turned and made her way along the corridor without any clear idea where she was going. She just knew that she'd had to get away from that inevitability she'd heard in Sean's voice, and from her own deep sense of regret which was, as he'd said, so fruitless.

Nothing could change what had happened, not today, not eight years ago. She had to live with the consequences of her actions. Suddenly, it seemed harder than ever to imagine doing that, to imagine living the rest of her life after Sean left.

The soft humming of bees in the nearby flowers was the only sound to disturb the silence. Claire sat on the bench with her face tilted up to the May sun. She could feel its warmth on her skin yet it didn't seem strong enough to penetrate the chill which had encased her for the past half-hour.

She had taken an early lunch-break, needing time to pull herself together after her conversation with Sean. The canteen had been crowded so she had bought herself a sandwich and carried it outside to the rose garden so that she could be by herself for a while.

She didn't want to have to speak to anyone until she was sure that she had herself under control. But how could she be sure of achieving that? Being around Sean, it seemed to have broken down the defensive wall with which she had surrounded herself these past years so that suddenly she felt swamped by all the emotions she had held in check for so long…

'So here you are. I've been looking for you.'

Sean's voice was little louder than the humming of the insects yet Claire reacted to it as though a cannon had gone off. She swung round, her eyes dilating with shock as she saw him standing a little way off.

He swore softly and Claire sensed both his anger and his frustration. No wonder! Sean had tried his best to make this situation as easy as possible for them but she wasn't helping him.

'I'm sorry…' she began huskily, only to stop as he gave a sharp downward thrust of his hand.

'Don't! Don't you dare say you're sorry, Claire. If there's anyone who needs to apologise then it's me. Why the hell didn't you tell me?'

'Tell you? What?' She stared at him in confusion, seeing myriad expressions cross his face without understanding a single one of them. 'Sean, I'm sorr—' she stopped when he looked at her. She glanced down and her voice was laced with confusion. 'I don't understand.'

'Neither did I, but that isn't any excuse! If I'd had any idea...' The anguish in his voice brought her eyes winging to his face. Claire felt her heart jolt as she saw the pain that was etched there.

He looked away as though he didn't want her to see how he was feeling, staring up at the sky as he ran a hand round the back of his neck. He had shed his white coat, before coming to find her, and the action made the thin fabric of his blue chambray shirt strain across the muscular width of his shoulders.

Claire felt her senses stir, felt the first small flutter of awareness grow until it turned into a churning knot in the pit of her stomach. Sean was so good-looking that no woman could be immune to him, yet she knew in her heart that her feelings were based on more than just physical attraction. Something inside him had always called to her as though they were two perfect halves of one whole. Eight years might have passed, both their lives might have changed, but that hadn't. It made her ache to realise it.

'Margaret just told me about Ben's father. You should have told me, Claire.'

She didn't know what to say and closed her eyes in an agony of indecision. Suddenly all the lies she had told seemed wrong, no matter that she had told them with the very best of intentions.

Oh, she could have glossed over the real facts by explaining that her relationship with Ben's father had ended for some reason or other. It wasn't unusual in this day and age and nobody would have thought anything about it. However, where would that have left Ben? One of the things she had wanted most for her son had been that he should have stability in his life, but how could he have had that if he'd been forever wondering when and if his father would turn up to see him—maybe ending up feeling rejected when it didn't happen?

She knew how that felt. After her own parents had divorced when she'd been ten, she could recall only too clearly the hours she'd spent waiting for her father to visit and how disappointed she'd been when he hadn't. It had seemed yet more proof that he hadn't cared about her.

It had taken her a long time to see that she hadn't been to blame, but the thought of Ben suffering the same heartache had been more than she could bear. It had been far better to tell Ben that his father was dead than let him keep on hoping.

'Margaret told me that he died of a heart attack,' Sean said softly.

Claire nodded, avoiding his eyes in case he saw how distraught she felt at having to perpetuate the lie. He muttered something harsh as he came and sat down beside her, but he didn't look at her as he hunched forward, his hands hanging loosely between his knee as he stared at the ground.

'No wonder it hit you hard, Finch dying like that,' he said with a wealth of sadness in his deep voice.

Claire swallowed the hard knot of tears that was clogging her throat, but her voice was choked when she spoke and she saw Sean look round. 'It...it's always sad when a patient dies.'

'Especially when it reminds you of your own loss.' He reached out and captured her hand, threading her slender fingers between his larger ones. Claire kept her gaze locked on their joined hands as she tried to fight the rush of awareness she felt, but just the sight of their hands linked was a sensual stimulant in its own way.

Her skin looked so pale in contrast to Sean's tan; her flesh felt so smooth and soft compared to the abrasiveness of his…

'Tell me about him, Claire. I want to know.'

She blanked out the dangerous swirl of sensations, concentrating instead on what she was going to say. Could she repeat the lies she had told in the past—even add to them? She'd been careful not to tell anyone more than she'd had to, hating having to lie even though she'd felt it necessary. Yet suddenly she knew that she couldn't bear to repeat it all to Sean.

She couldn't lie to him about something so important! Yet wasn't the truth equally impossible to tell? What would he do if she suddenly told him that there had been no other man and that…that Ben was his son?

She drew her hand away and stood up, overwhelmed by fear at the thought of how he might react. Maybe it was only a slim risk, but the thought of ever losing Ben if Sean fought her for custody was too big to take. 'I…I don't want to talk about it. It's over and done with.'

His eyes blazed yet they held a sadness which almost made her cry out as he stood up. 'Is it, Claire? Is it over? Or do you not want to talk about it because you're still so in love with him that you can't bear to face the fact that he's dead?' He gave a soft laugh, the sound seeming to be drawn from somewhere deep inside him.

'God knows, I understand how that feels! I know what it's like to try to avoid thinking about something that's so painful it tears you in two. But at the end of the day there's no way to avoid it. The pain is always with you. You might try your best to forget but in your heart you know that nothing on this earth can ever make you forget such a loss.'

He turned and walked away without waiting for her to answer. Claire watched him go until the sun dazzled her eyes so that she could no longer see clearly. She took a small gulping breath, feeling the pain tightening like a tourniquet around her heart.

Had Sean lost someone *he* had loved? It was the only explanation for that note of anguish in his voice. Yet the thought was so painful that she shied away from it.

She didn't want to think about the woman Sean had loved and lost, to wonder who she was and what had happened. Imagining Sean loving another woman was more than she could bear...even now.

CHAPTER FIVE

'I'M ANTHEA Berry. You have my son here… Simon…'

Claire was passing through Reception on her way back from lunch when she heard the woman's voice. She made her way to the desk, nodding to June behind the counter. 'I'll see to this, thanks, June.'

She turned to Anthea Berry, her heart going out to her as she saw the fear on her face. 'I'm Sister Shepherd, Mrs Berry. Will you come with me, please, and I'll get the doctor to have a word with you about Simon?'

'How is he? What happened? The policeman said he'd been in some sort of car accident!' The woman pressed a hand to her mouth to hold back a sob. 'He isn't… isn't…?'

Claire shook her head. 'No. Your son is alive, Mrs Berry. He's badly injured but he's alive.' She opened the door to the relatives' room and ushered the distraught woman inside.

'I don't understand how it happened.' Anthea sank onto a chair. She looked at Claire with the eyes of someone who still hadn't grasped what was happening. 'Simon went off to school, as he usually does, at about eight-thirty. It was only a couple of weeks before the Easter holiday that I started letting him walk there on his own. He kept going on and on about me not treating him like a baby now that he's nearly nine…' She swallowed. 'But he's always so careful about crossing the road. That's what I can't understand!'

Claire chose her words with care. The police would

be the ones to inform Simon's mother of the full circumstances surrounding the accident. 'I don't think it was Simon's fault, Mrs Berry. From what I can gather, the car came round the corner too fast to avoid him.'

'Oh, my Lord!' Tears ran down the woman's face. 'I should have been there! It's all my fault…'

Claire took her hand in an instinctive gesture of comfort, trying not to think about how Sean had done the same thing to her just a short time before. 'You mustn't blame yourself. It was a dreadful accident. You must concentrate on Simon now. I'll go and find Dr Fitzgerald so that he can explain…'

She glanced round as the door opened then rose to her feet, feeling the heat that ran through her body as Sean came into the room. His face gave little away as he nodded to her, yet she knew instinctively that what had happened in the rose garden was still very much on his mind.

'June told me that Mrs Berry was here. I thought I'd just come and tell her how Simon is.'

'I was just about to get you,' Claire said quietly as she moved aside so that Sean could take the chair opposite the child's mother. He sat down, reaching over to take Mrs Berry's hands, and Claire was struck once again by his compassion for the people he dealt with. Not even the tragedies he had seen in recent years had changed that because it was an intrinsic part of him. It had been another of the things she had loved about him…

She cut short the unsettling thought, listening silently as Sean quietly explained about Simon's injuries. 'Simon is undergoing an operation to remove fragments of broken bone from inside his skull. Once that has been done we'll have a clearer picture of how badly injured he is.

He also has a broken pelvis and some lacerations to his face, which will be dealt with.'

'And…and after this operation? What then, Doctor? Will Simon be all right?' Mrs Berry's voice broke. 'He won't be brain damaged, will he? My baby will get better?'

Sean sighed as he squeezed her hands. 'We just can't say at this stage, Mrs Berry. The prognosis for this type of injury is always difficult. All we can do is wait and pray that things will turn out as we all hope they will. Everything possible will be done to help Simon. I promise you that.'

He broke off as the door burst open. He stood up as a man appeared, not needing Mrs Berry's cry of relief to tell him that this was Simon's father.

'I only just got the message, Anthea. What happened? Where is he?'

Claire led the way from the room, leaving the distraught parents to have a few moments on their own. She sighed as Sean closed the door. 'I always wish there was something more we could do at a time like this, but there isn't anything you can say, is there?'

Sean shook his head. 'No. The only thing they want to hear is that their son is going to be all right, and it just isn't possible to promise them that yet awhile.' He looked at Claire and his gaze was pensive. 'I imagine it hits home even harder when you have a child of your own, Claire.'

'It does. Simon goes to the same school Ben goes to. Why, he's almost the same age—' She broke off, wondering if it had been wise to mention that. However, Sean appeared not to have noticed the betraying slip she'd made.

She gave him a thin smile then quickly excused herself and hurried away. Her heart was beating wildly as she set about restocking the shelves in the trauma unit. It was a task she usually delegated to one of the junior nurses but she chose to do it herself so that she could have a few minutes on her own.

She laid sterile dressings in their proper places, checked sutures and fetched another chest-drain set from the supply cupboard. Still her heart kept hammering away. What if Sean remembered what she'd said—would he start adding things up? It wouldn't take much working out to realise that her son must have been conceived during the time they had been together. A little basic addition and all the lies she had told would go up in smoke. It wasn't complicated. One plus one equalled the right answer. Claire plus Sean equalled Ben! What on earth was she going to do?

'This is Emma Daly. She's ten months old and has been vomiting since lunchtime. Her mother is also worried because she appears to be constipated.'

'Right, let's have a look at her.' Sean smiled at the anxious mother then turned his attention to the little girl, who was crying listlessly. Claire gently caught hold of the baby's flailing hands and held them out of the way as Sean examined her.

'Hmm, there are definite signs of swelling in the abdomen and obviously Emma is in some pain.' He glanced at the child's mother. 'How long is it since Emma passed a motion, Mrs Daly?'

'Not since last night, Doctor.' Mrs Daly ran a soothing hand over her daughter's wispy brown curls. 'I haven't had a dirty nappy since then, although when I changed her just a while ago I noticed that there was blood in her nappy. That's why I brought her straight here, you see.'

'You did the right thing,' Sean assured her, then glanced at Claire. 'The bowel is obviously obstructed. I'd guess it's an intussusception, from what Mrs Daly has said. The symptoms are spot on—pain, vomiting, constipation and swelling of the abdomen, plus a blood-stained mucus discharged from the bowels.'

'Shall I ring through to Paediatrics? Or are you going to deal with it here with a barium enema?' Claire queried softly, not wanting to alarm the baby's mother too much.

Intussusception was a condition which predominantly affected infants. It occurred when part of the intestine telescoped inside itself. She recalled Dr Hill explaining it to her once when another child had been brought in with the same symptoms. He had likened it to what happened when a tightly fitting glove was drawn off the hand and one of the fingers turned partly inside out, and she had never heard a better description.

Sean nodded. His expression was appreciative as he returned her look. 'The latter, I think, Claire, don't you?'

'I'll just get what you need, then.' Claire busied herself collecting what would be needed as Sean quietly explained to the baby's mother what he intended to do. She tried to focus all her attention on what she was doing but she couldn't deny the small glow of warmth inside her as she recalled the way he had included her in the decision about how they would treat baby Emma.

It was nice to be appreciated and nice to know that Sean valued her contribution. She had always prided herself on her professionalism because nursing was more than just a job to her. But medicine had always been more than just a job to Sean as well. They would have made a good team, she and Sean, if they'd gone to

Africa together. But then, they would have made a good team in their private lives as well as their professional ones.

It was too painful to dwell on that so Claire busied herself with the task at hand. Prompt treatment was essential and hydrostatic reduction of the intussusception by means of a barium enema would hopefully work. If it didn't then Emma would need surgery to remove the obstruction, but Claire was hoping it wouldn't come to that.

It all took some time but it did work. By the time Emma was being wheeled up to Paediatrics, where she would stay overnight for observation, the evening staff had come on duty. Claire had a few reassuring words with Mrs Daly, who intended to spend the night at Emma's bedside, then went to the office to give her report.

Most of the day staff had left by the time she collected her things from the staffroom, although Sean's coat was still tossed over a chair, she noticed. He never seemed in a hurry to leave like the rest of them. It made her wonder where he was living and if he had rented a flat or taken lodgings.

He would be in Dalverston such a short time that it wouldn't have been worth him looking for anywhere permanent. His contract was for three months and where he would go after that was open to speculation.

Would he return to Africa? she wondered. Or would he remain in England a while longer?

She sighed as she left the building. She had to stop thinking about him all the time! Granted, it wasn't easy, with them being thrown daily into such close proximity, but she had her own life to lead, a life which would carry on when Sean had gone. What he did or didn't do was his business!

Squaring her shoulders, Claire made her way to the car park, glad that her car hadn't needed an expensive repair in the end. A flat battery had caused the problem but an overnight charge had soon sorted it out. Now, as she backed out of the parking space, she realised that she had better stop off at the supermarket on her way home. Remembering the empty fridge, it was more a necessity than a choice!

The supermarket was crowded with evening shoppers. Claire wheeled her trolley up and down the aisles, collecting what she needed as quickly as possible. She could have done with having a really good shop but she didn't want to keep Mrs Mitchell waiting too long for her to get back, so she contented herself with just picking up the basics. She was checking that she had everything she needed when she came to the end of an aisle and gasped in dismay as she cannoned into another trolley coming in the opposite direction.

'Oops, sorry… Sean!' Claire couldn't hide her surprise as she saw who was pushing the other trolley. Sean gave her a broad grin, his blue eyes sparkling with amusement.

'I hope you pay more attention when you're driving.'

She blushed despite the teasing note in his voice, or maybe because of it, she acknowledged. It made her feel warm inside to hear him speak to her like that and recall other times he'd teased her unmercifully in the past.

She avoided his eyes, afraid that he'd guess what she was thinking. 'I'm a lot more careful out on the roads, believe me. I was just checking to see what I'd forgotten and didn't notice you.'

'Doesn't look to me like you've forgotten very much.'

His brows rose comically as he shot a meaningful glance from her trolley to his, and Claire couldn't help but laugh. Her 'basics' had added up to a small mountain of goods while Sean's shopping consisted of a bottle of wine and a few microwave dinners.

She picked up a packet of ready-to-serve chicken tikka with rice, and grimaced. 'You really like this stuff?'

'No, not really.' He shrugged. 'It's the easy option, that's all.'

'You used to love cooking,' she said without thinking. 'Remember all the meals you used to make for us and how adventurous you were experimenting with all sorts of recipes?' She looked up with a smile, which faded abruptly as she saw the expression in his eyes.

'I remember, Claire. I'm surprised you do, though.' His voice was very deep and held a wealth of meaning. She took a deep breath but it didn't ease the pain as the memories swirled through her mind. Her brown eyes were clouded as they met his blue ones in a look neither of them seemed inclined to break by saying anything. But maybe they didn't need to say anything. Perhaps all it needed was this one shared moment to say all that was necessary?

'Excuse me!'

An indignant voice cut through the silence. Claire stepped aside to let the woman pass, using the few seconds it took to regain her composure, but it wasn't easy to ignore the sadness she felt at recalling all those wonderful times she and Sean had spent together.

'We seem to be holding up traffic, don't we? Have you got everything you need?'

'I think so.' She stared blankly down at her trolley then jumped when he touched her arm. Her eyes flew to his and it was still there, that same expression in his eyes. It shook her to know that Sean remembered those days as clearly as she did. Somehow she had never expected that.

'There's a till free over there.' He slid his hand under her arm, guiding her towards the empty checkout. Claire took a deep breath yet she could feel the flurries his touch was arousing running under her skin. She was glad when she was able to move away to unload her shopping, but all it took was the brushing of their hands as he bent to help her to set loose another flurry.

'Here, I'll unload while you pack.' Sean casually edged her out of the way as he bent to the task. Claire hesitated but it seemed ridiculous to make a fuss over something so trivial. It took half the time to get everything sorted out and paid for, with two of them doing the job, so it seemed churlish not to wait and help him pack his shopping.

They left the supermarket together and, as luck would have it, Sean had parked near her car. He waited for her to unlock the boot then insisted on lifting the bags into it, despite her protests.

'Some of these are heavy, Claire. You shouldn't be lifting them. Right, that's the lot.'

He snapped the boot lid shut then looked at her. There was a slight breeze blowing that evening and it whipped his hair over his forehead in a tangle of blue-black curls. Claire's hands clenched against an urge to brush it back. She fixed a stiff little smile to her mouth, praying that he wouldn't guess how she was feeling, so on edge and aware of him that her whole body seemed to be tingling.

'Well, thanks for your help, Sean. I appreciate it. I'm sorry if I've delayed you.'

'I'm in no rush to get home.' He cast a disparaging

glance at the frozen dinners. 'Mmm, I wonder which of these I should have tonight? The chicken or the prawn curry? Hard to decide between two such culinary feasts, isn't it?'

She laughed tightly, not wanting any more reminders of the meals they had shared in the past. 'It certainly is.' She cast round for something to say that wouldn't hold too many pitfalls. 'Where are you living, by the way? Have you found a flat?'

'A house, no less. Juliet Carmichael, who was working in A and E before me, wanted to rent it out so I took advantage of her offer.' He shrugged. 'From what I can gather, she's thinking about selling up as she's decided to move back to London. She's got a job with a pharmaceutical company there, in the sales department. She's decided that medicine isn't for her.'

'What a shame!' Claire sighed. 'Although I can't blame her because it isn't an easy job, is it?'

'No. But when is anything worthwhile ever easy?' Sean shrugged. 'Anyhow, I'm renting the place while she makes up her mind what she intends to do with it. It suits me fine, although I do rattle around a bit in all those empty rooms. Still, once my family discovers I've got no less than three spare bedrooms I'm sure they'll be happy to fill them!'

Claire laughed at that. Sean was one of four brothers, and she recalled only too well the nights when they had all met up for an impromptu party. 'How are they all? As crazy as ever?'

'Worse!' Sean laughed. 'They're all married *and* they've all got children. Can you imagine what it's like when the whole lot descends on my parents at Christmas? I thought the roof was going to fly off last time! Mind you, Mum enjoyed every second of it.'

Claire frowned. 'So you haven't just come back to England, then? You were home for Christmas?'

'Oh, yes.' He looked down, deliberately avoiding her eyes so that she had a feeling there was something he didn't want her to know. 'I've been back in England for almost a year now, doing temporary work while I decide what I want to do next.'

He looked up suddenly and shrugged, and there was a bleakness in his eyes which belied his seeming nonchalance. 'I was thinking about staying on but I'll probably go back, if not to Africa then maybe India. They're crying out for doctors there at present.'

'I see.' Claire toyed with her car keys, trying to stave off a feeling of emptiness at the thought of him living on the other side of the world in a few weeks' time. 'Well, it was what you wanted most, wasn't it? To work with the underprivileged?'

She looked up and felt a ripple of shock run through her as she saw the way his eyes blazed before his lids lowered abruptly. What was behind it? she wondered dizzily. Why had he looked at her like that? Yet when he answered his tone was devoid of emotion, making her wonder if she had imagined the brief display of passion.

'Yes, it was what I always wanted, Claire.' He reached into the trolley and picked up the packet of prawn curry. 'Right, I've decided. It's going to be this little culinary masterpiece tonight. Yummy!'

His tone was deliberately teasing and she laughed dutifully, realising that he was trying to lighten the rather sombre mood. 'I'd say lucky you, only it would be a lie!'

'Well, in the absence of home cooking…' His expression was comical but that didn't mean she missed the hint he was giving her. She took a quick breath, wondering if she was completely crazy not to ignore it…

'Why don't you come and have tea with us?' The words had come out before she could stop them and, once they were said, she could hardly take them back. Her pulse began to race as she realised what she had done so that it took her all her time to continue with a modicum of composure.

'I can't promise anything fancy but I'm sure it will be better than one of those frozen dinners.'

'Are you sure?' Sean's gaze was intent. He smiled when she nodded, his blue eyes lighting up with genuine pleasure. 'Then thank you, Claire. I'd like that very much indeed. Shall I follow you back or do you want me to come round a bit later?' he suggested thoughtfully.

'You…you may as well follow me home. Ben's always starving when he gets in from school, so I daren't make him wait for his tea or I could have a mutiny on my hands!' she replied, trying to inject a little levity into her voice.

'Great. Just give me a minute to put these in the boot and then you can lead on.'

Sean strode to his car and packed his shopping away. Claire got into her car and started the engine, aware that her heart was hammering. She took a deep breath then she backed out of the parking space. It was just an invitation to tea, that was all, something she had issued to several of her colleagues, she told herself sternly as she headed for the exit. Nothing untoward would happen because Ben would be there…

In the circumstances, that wasn't the best thought to calm her fears. She groaned as she glanced in her rear-view mirror and saw Sean wave to her. What had she done?

CHAPTER SIX

'GOAL! That's six to me and one to you, Sean! Wipe-out!'

Ben's delighted cry carried clearly to the kitchen where Claire was washing up, and she smiled wistfully. Her son had taken an immediate liking to Sean from the moment they had been introduced. Ben was normally shy about meeting strangers, and about meeting men in particular, as he wasn't used to a male presence in his life. However, there had been no hesitation as he'd chatted to Sean over tea, telling him about his favourite subjects at school. It was incredibly poignant in the circumstances to see how quickly the pair had developed such a rapport.

'Need a hand with those dishes?'

She quickly smoothed her face into a suitable expression as Sean suddenly appeared, wishing that it weren't necessary. How marvellous it would be if there was no more need to pretend. They could act like a real family then, just a mother and a father playing happily with their son…

She looked away as she felt the hot sting of tears behind her eyelids, focusing all her attention on drying the plate she'd just washed. 'No, it's fine, really. You go and keep Ben company. Sounds as though you're having fun in there.'

'We were, but I could do with an excuse to escape, to be honest. It's rather a strain, having to keep up a front.'

Her eyes shot to his face. 'Keep up a front… What do you mean?'

'That it doesn't do much for the old ego, getting well and truly trounced like that! You never warned me that child of yours is a champion Subbuteo player, Claire. He's just annihilated me!' Sean grinned but there was concern in his eyes as he saw how pale she had gone.

She took a quick breath, struggling to regain her composure. For a horrible moment there… She blanked out the rest of that thought and managed a laugh which sounded at least halfway normal. 'Mmm, surely you're big enough to take defeat gracefully? I keep telling Ben that you have to lose sometimes…'

'I should have known I wouldn't get any sympathy! You're a hard woman, Claire Shepherd.' He laughed as he took the teatowel from her and began drying the dishes. 'Anyway, Ben's a great kid, Claire. You've done a fantastic job of bringing him up, although it can't have been easy on your own.'

'Thank you,' she replied softly, lifting a pan from the stove so that he wouldn't see how much the compliment had touched her. 'I suppose it has been hard at times, but having Ben has made it all worthwhile. I don't know what I would do without him.'

Sean stacked the dry plate on top of the pile of clean ones and sighed. 'I envy you, you know? Oh, I realise that the situation isn't ideal, but having a child must give a very special purpose to your life.'

It was impossible to hold back the tears as he said that because it was just too poignant to be reminded of how different things might have been. Claire stared down at the soapy water, praying that he wouldn't notice how upset she was, but, of course, he did.

He tossed the cloth onto the table and turned her to

face him, uncaring that she was dripping soapsuds all down his shirt front. 'What is it, Claire? What did I say?'

He stopped abruptly as a look of contrition crossed his face. 'I'm so sorry! What a stupid, thoughtless thing to say.' He put his hand under her chin, gently forcing her to meet his eyes. 'I never meant to hurt you by reminding you about what you've lost, sweetheart. It must be dreadful for you, watching Ben growing up into such a fine little boy and knowing that his father can't be here to share in all the joy he brings you. I'm sorry, Claire…so very, very sorry.'

It was just too much. She gave a choked sob as all the emotion she'd been holding in check since Sean had arrived in Dalverston suddenly spilled over. Tears ran unchecked down her cheeks and she heard the anguished exclamation he gave as he drew her into his arms.

'Shh, shh. Don't cry, love. It's all right, everything will be all right.' His voice was so deep and resonant with emotion as he tried to soothe her that she just cried all the harder. He drew her even closer, nestling her head against his shoulder as he smoothed her hair with a hand that wasn't quite steady.

'Don't, Claire. I can't bear to see you crying like this and know that I'm to blame!'

There was such raw agony in his voice that her eyes lifted to his, despite her anguish, and what she saw made her heart pound. Sean was looking at her as though he would have given everything he possessed if it would have stopped her being upset.

His deep voice grated as he raised a shaking hand to wipe away her tears. 'I'm sorry, Claire. I wish that things could have been different…for both of us.'

'What do you mean?' she whispered shakily, even though she knew it was foolish to ask. Both their emotions were so raw at that moment that it was dangerous to ask questions like that. But suddenly she had to know what was behind the pain she saw in his eyes. 'Tell me, Sean.'

He took a deep breath yet his voice rasped even more hoarsely. 'That if I hadn't been so selfish and set on going overseas then maybe that boy in there could have been my son! Maybe I shouldn't be saying this, Claire, but I can't help it. You loved me. I know you did! But I asked too much of you, didn't I? What woman in her right mind would have willingly opted for the kind of life I was offering you?'

His hand rested on her cheek so that she shivered as she felt the long, strong fingers against her skin. 'Ben could have been my child, couldn't he, Claire? Please, tell me I'm right.'

What could she say? To deny it was more than she could bear in the face of his grief. She closed her eyes, terrified that she would blurt out the truth if she looked at him a moment longer.

'Yes, Sean,' she whispered shakily. 'Ben c-could have been your son if…if things had been different.'

He became so tense that she could feel every muscle in his body going rigid before he abruptly let her go. He went to the table and stood with his head bowed so that she couldn't see his face. Claire knew that he was struggling for control and the urge to go to him was so great that it was unbearable. Sean was hurting so much that all she wanted at that moment was to comfort him in any way she could!

She took a step towards him then stopped as Ben came racing into the kitchen.

'Hey, Sean, do you want a game of football in the

garden? Mum's promised that I can have new football boots for my birthday and I need to practise,' he said eagerly.

'Sean might not feel like playing any more games with you,' Claire cut in quickly, glancing at Sean so that she saw the deep breath he took before he straightened. He gave her a quick smile before he turned to Ben, but she could see the effort it cost him to act naturally for the child's benefit and her heart ached even more for what he was going through and what she was doing.

She had it in her power to erase that grief she had seen in his eyes with a few simple words, but could she do it? Could she take the risk? It was the uncertainty of not knowing what would happen that kept her silent, that and the need to protect Ben. How could she destroy Ben's safe little world by admitting that she had told him a pack of lies when he was too young to understand the reason for them?

She took a deep breath, knowing that it was a risk she couldn't take to relieve her guilt or even assuage Sean's pain. Ben's needs had to come first because he was the really vulnerable one in all of this.

'Well, it depends,' Sean said with mock severity, making a determined effort to stop the child guessing that anything was wrong. 'If you're intending to make this another wipeout then I don't know whether I can face it. Being beaten twice in one night might be more than I can stand!'

Ben laughed gleefully, blissfully unaware of the undercurrents. 'I'll give you a start, then. You can have two goals for free. How's that?'

'Sounds fair enough to me, not that I'm expecting to win after my last showing, though!' He smiled as Ben whooped with delight then hurried off to find his football. However, his smile faded as he turned to Claire and there was an expression in his eyes that made her become tense in her turn.

'Thank you for what you said just now, Claire. I know I had no right to ask such a question but I appreciate your honesty more than I can tell you. You may find it hard to understand but somehow it makes things easier to deal with.'

She was spared having to reply as Ben arrived back with the ball just then. She quietly warned him not to race around too much in case it set off an asthma attack, although it had been ages since he'd had one.

'Don't worry, Claire. I'll make sure he doesn't get too excited.' Sean laid a protective hand on the boy's shoulder as he gave a rueful smile. 'Not that he'll need to race around much, with me on the opposing team, of course. He'll probably beat me hollow just by standing still!'

Ben giggled happily at that and was still laughing as he and Sean went into the garden. Claire stood by the window and watched them, knowing that she would remember this moment all her life. To see her son playing with his father, it was a memory which would be stored in her heart for ever, although it could never make up for the sadness she felt, or the guilt. Sean had been wrong because he had nothing to be grateful to her for. She just hadn't had the courage to be completely honest with him, and that was the burden she would have to live with for the rest of her days.

'Now, straight to sleep, young man. No reading tonight. It's way past your bedtime.' Claire tucked the duvet round her son then kissed him on the cheek. 'Night-night, sleep tight. Mind the bugs—'

'Don't bite,' Ben finished the familiar refrain for her,

grinning happily. 'Can Sean come to tea again, Mum? Please? It's been brilliant tonight!'

'We'll see. Now, go to sleep!'

She closed the door then went downstairs. Sean was in the sitting-room, listening to a record she'd put on the old stereo. He looked up as she came into the room and smiled at her.

'In bed at last? I don't know where he gets his energy from. I'm shattered!'

'Me, too.' Claire laughed nervously as she bent down to switch on another lamp. It was after nine and the evening was growing dark. She had turned on a lamp before going upstairs, but the soft glow it gave out made the room look rather too intimately cosy in her opinion.

Oddly enough, things had settled down after the earlier outpouring of emotion. Whether that was because Sean had gone out of his way to keep the mood light or because Ben had been around, she wasn't sure. But, surprisingly, she had found herself able to relax and enjoy the rest of the evening.

Sean was good company and a lot of fun, taking an obvious delight in teasing Ben as they'd played a madcap game of snap. Ben had positively blossomed under the attention, losing all traces of his usual reserve. It was obvious that Sean had a way with children and didn't make the mistake of trying to talk down to the boy, as so many people did.

Claire had enjoyed watching the interaction between the pair, even though it had been so poignant to see. Now, however, she wasn't sorry when Sean got up because she was suddenly overwhelmingly conscious of how quiet it was now that Ben was in bed. Perhaps it would be better to put an end to an evening, which had run the whole gamut of emotions, before it ran any more.

'I think I'd better be off. I don't want to outstay my welcome.' He groaned exaggeratedly as he eased the stiffness out of his muscles, saving her from having to think up some polite reply. 'Oh, am I going to pay for being mad enough to play that extra game of football! I should have accepted the fact that I'm getting a bit long in the tooth for such activities.'

'Oh, mind you don't trip over your beard, Methuselah!' she teased, relieved to take her cue from him.

'Cheeky monkey! And here I was keeping your son entertained, too.' He gave her a crooked grin which made her heart turn over. 'It's been a great night, Claire. I can't remember when I enjoyed myself so much.'

'Good. Th—that's what I like to hear.' She turned away, not wanting him to see how that smile had affected her. She led the way to the front door, struggling to keep her emotions in check, but her pulse was racing like crazy all of a sudden. Her hand shook as she opened the door then stepped back so that Sean could pass her.

He paused on the bottom step, his blue eyes playing over her face in a way that simply increased her nervousness. Was it her imagination or was that hunger she saw in his eyes real?

She lowered her eyes, afraid of what the answer might be. There was no going back! What she and Sean had felt about one another was over and it would be foolish to allow the situation to develop into anything other than the friendship he had suggested. She should be grateful if they could achieve that, yet as she looked at him again she knew in her heart that she would have liked much more than friendship if things had been different.

'I'll say goodnight, then. And thank you again for a lovely evening.'

The husky warmth in his voice sent a little ripple down her spine. Her hand tightened on the lock as she struggled to control it, but it seemed to be spreading to other parts of her body at a rate of knots. When Sean suddenly bent and kissed her cheek she gave a small gasp and immediately drew back, then felt the colour flood her face as she saw his surprise. He didn't say anything, however, simply walked down the path and waved before getting into his car.

Claire stayed on the step until the car's red taillights had faded into the night. She pressed the tips of her fingers to the spot on her cheek where his lips had touched it, feeling how her skin still tingled.

It had been just a token, that was all, the sort of social kiss which people gave one another all the time. It would be foolish to read anything more into it, foolish *and* dangerous. Her head told her that but her heart…well, her heart couldn't help wishing for all sorts of foolish things!

'Is Simon Berry going to be all right, Mum?'

Claire looked up from packing sandwiches into Ben's lunchbox, and sighed. It was three days since Simon had been brought into hospital, three days since Sean had come to tea, and the time seemed to have flown past. She had seen him each day at work, of course, and he had treated her with a casual friendliness which had both reassured and irritated her.

She was glad that he seemed determined to keep things on an even keel between them, especially after what he'd said about wishing Ben had been his son. But sometimes it annoyed her that he seemed to find it less of a strain than she did. Where Sean was concerned it seemed that her feelings constantly veered in opposite directions!

'We don't know yet, darling. Simon was still unconscious when I left work last night, I'm afraid,' she replied, determinedly focusing her mind on what the child had said rather than her own jumbled thoughts. 'He could remain that way for some time yet.'

Ben spooned up another mouthful of cereal and chewed it thoughtfully. 'But he'll be OK when he wakes up, won't he?'

Claire snapped the lid on the plastic box and went to get a yoghurt out of the fridge, wondering how best to explain Simon's condition. She didn't want to say too much about their fears for Simon's recovery, but it seemed wrong to let Ben think that it was as simple as he imagined.

She sat down at the table and looked gravely at him. 'All the doctors are trying their very best to make Simon better, but there's no way they can tell how badly hurt he is at the moment. When he does wake up they'll have a better idea of how long it will be before he's well again. But it will take some time, Ben.'

'I see. I wish I was a doctor. I'd make people better,' Ben said resolutely. He looked at Claire and she felt her heart turn inside out at the familiarity of the direct blue stare. 'I wouldn't let anyone stay hurt if I could help them!'

'I...I'm sure you wouldn't, darling.' She stood up abruptly, turning away so that Ben couldn't see the tears in her eyes. Her son had both looked and sounded so like Sean just then that it had made her heart ache. Children inherited so much from their parents and the thought that Ben might have inherited Sean's desire to help people made her both proud and sad...

'Is that why my daddy wanted to be a doctor, because he wanted to stop people from hurting?'

She only just managed to contain her gasp as Ben asked the question right out of the blue. She glanced round, wondering if he had picked up on her thoughts somehow. Ben rarely spoke about his father and that he should have done so now seemed very strange.

'Yes,' she replied quietly. 'Your father is...was a wonderful doctor. His whole aim in life was to help as many people as he could.'

She just managed to stop herself making the slip and thankfully Ben appeared not to have noticed that she had moved from present to past tense in the same breath. He spooned the last of the cereal from his bowl then carried it over to the sink, his small face set into a frown.

'Do you think my father would have been able to make Simon better, Mum? I bet he could!'

Claire managed to smile but it took every scrap of determination she possessed. 'I'm sure he would have tried his hardest, darling. Now, run along and fetch your schoolbag or you'll be late.'

Ben went rushing out of the kitchen while Claire ran water into the bowl to wash their dishes, feeling the pain settling deep into her heart. It had never been easy to lie to Ben and now it seemed doubly difficult. Oh, she'd told him as much as she'd dared, that his father had been a doctor. She'd even told him about Sean's dreams of working overseas so that Ben could build up a picture of him. However, it no longer seemed enough when she found herself wondering if she'd had the *right* to deny Sean and Ben such an important part of both their lives.

Could she and Sean have found a way to deal with the situation rather than the extreme solution she had decided on? Had her fears been groundless all those years ago?

She sighed as she turned off the tap. What was the point of thinking 'what if'? What was done was done. Now she had to make the best of it…and telling Ben or Sean the truth wasn't the way!

'Help me…please, someone, help!'

There was such panic in the young woman's voice that Claire stopped dead. She swung round in time to see Margaret racing out of the doors. Abandoning her plans to go to the canteen for an early lunch, she hurriedly followed.

The morning had been hectic from the moment she had come on duty to discover that two of the junior nurses were off sick. It had left them with a seriously depleted staff so that they had been hard-pressed to cope with the stream of patients who had appeared.

Lunch-breaks were having to be staggered to maintain cover, but even then they were on the borderline of coping. All it would take was one big emergency and the whole department would grind to a halt. Hopefully, this wasn't going to be it!

She hurried outside to find Margaret crouched beside a battered old Mini, which was parked all askew in front of the doors. She could see little, apart from Margaret's back and the frantic face of the young woman who had called for assistance.

'What's happened?' she asked firmly, putting a stop to the girl's hysterics by her very calmness.

'It's David. He…he just went all…all *peculiar*!'

The girl ran the back of her hand over her tear-streaked face as she looked uncertainly at the car. Claire left her for a moment and crouched down beside Margaret to see what was going on.

'How is he?' she asked quietly.

'He seems a bit disorientated. And there's a nasty cut on his head. But his pulse and breathing are OK,' Margaret replied over her shoulder.

'We need to get him inside but I doubt we'll manage it by ourselves,' Claire replied. 'You stay with him, Margaret, while I get a porter and see what else his girlfriend can tell us.'

Leaving Margaret to keep the patient calm, Claire took hold of the girl's arm and led her inside the building. 'When you say ''peculiar'', what do you mean exactly?' she probed gently.

The girl grimaced. 'I don't know… It's hard to explain. We…we were just having a laugh, you know. David was chasing me and then all of a sudden he gave this funny sort of moan and fell down. He was all stiff at first and then he started jerking about…' She gulped, looking very much as though she was going to pass out herself. Claire gave her a moment to compose herself then urged her on.

'And how did he get that cut on his head? Before or after he fell?'

'After. Well, during, actually. He hit his head on the cupboard when he fell,' the girl explained. 'I don't know if it's that or what happened before, but he doesn't seem to know where he is or what's going on!'

'I see. The best thing you can do right now is go to the desk and give the receptionist David's details while we bring him inside.' Claire smiled encouragingly as she hesitated. 'Can you do that?'

'I don't know.' The girl blushed. 'I don't know him that well, you see. We only started going out together a couple of weeks ago. I'm not sure if I can tell you what you need to know.'

'Just do your best.' Claire gave her a gentle push towards the desk then asked one of the porters to fetch a trolley. Sean had just finished dealing with a patient and he stopped her as she passed.

'Problems?' he queried. Claire paused, noticing all of a sudden how tired he looked. She had found herself working alongside Dr Hill for most of the morning so had only come into brief contact with Sean that day. Now she couldn't help but see the shadows under his eyes which hinted at a restless night.

Had Sean been lying awake, thinking about what had happened the other evening? she wondered suddenly. The thought that it might have been preying on his mind as much as on hers was something of a mixed blessing, and she hastily rid herself of it before it could do any more damage.

She quickly outlined all she knew about the man in the car then headed back to the forecourt with Sean at her side. Margaret looked relieved when they appeared, closely followed by the porter with a trolley.

'At last. I was beginning to think you'd gone sick as well!' she observed tartly.

'Sorry. I was just explaining to Sean what the girl told me.' Claire bent down to look at the young man who was slumped in the passenger seat. 'How is he?'

'A bit groggy.' Margaret informed them. 'His name's David Duggan and he's twenty-two. I got that much out of him, but he can't remember his address or what happened.'

'Let's get him inside, then.' Sean took charge, and between them they soon managed to get the patient out of the car and onto the trolley.

Claire led the way to a free cubicle then glanced at Margaret. 'Can you take your lunch-break now? I was on my way to the canteen but I'll hang on here.'

'Of course. No problem.' Margaret gave her an old-fashioned look. 'You stay and help Sean, Claire.'

Margaret gave her a cheeky grin and headed off towards the lift. Claire drew the curtain across, trying to pretend that she wasn't blushing. Had Margaret sensed something from the way she'd been acting around Sean? Or had it been a lucky guess? Her friend was an incorrigible matchmaker at the best of times so it was hard to tell. But the thought that she might have been acting differently around Sean, and had aroused other people's suspicions, didn't sit too easily with her.

'I just want to look into your eyes, David. Lie back and try to relax.' Sean's tone was at it's most soothing but it appeared to be having little effect, Claire realised. She hurried to the bed and laid a restraining hand on the young man's shoulder as he tried to sit up, glad to concentrate on her work rather than such unsettling thoughts.

'Now, do as Dr Fitzgerald says, David. Just try to relax. We only want to help you.' She added her encouragement but it had even less effect. The young man's face was set into belligerent lines as he tried to push her away.

'I'm fine. I don't need a doctor. I want to leave.' He swung his legs over the side of the bed and stood up before either of them could stop him.

'Catch him!' Sean shouted as David's legs gave way. He took the man's weight as Claire hurried round the bed to help get the patient back onto the trolley.

She quickly raised the safety bars either side to stop David from trying to get up a second time. However, he was lying limply against the pillows now, with tears trickling down his face.

Sean shot her a puzzled glance, obviously as confused as she was by such odd behavior. However, his tone was perfectly even as he returned to the task of examining the patient. 'I just want to check you over, David. All right?'

'There's no need. I can tell you what's wrong.' David said thickly. 'I had a fit. You know, epilepsy?' He gave a hoarse laugh. 'Take my word for it, Doctor, that's what happened!'

'I see. So you've had it happen before, have you?' Sean folded his arms and looked levelly at him. 'When was the last time, do you remember?'

'Oh, I remember all right. Two years and three months ago exactly,' David informed them bitterly. 'I marked it on my calendar, you see, and I've been counting the days since it happened. I'd just convinced myself that I wasn't going to have another one and put in to take my driving test. Fat chance of that now!'

'I know it's hard but nowadays epilepsy can be controlled to a far greater degree than it could be in the past.' Sean said quietly. 'It needn't be the handicap it used to be or carry the same stigma.'

'Fine words, Doc. But you try convincing other people of that!' David sounded angry. 'You've no idea what it feels like to wake up and find a whole load of strangers staring at you as though you're some sort of bloody freak show!'

'I don't suppose I have. But if you allow it to ruin your life then it will. OK, so it's embarrassing—I can understand that. But it can be controlled. The fact that you went all that time without having a seizure proves that,' Sean said sternly. Claire wondered if he wasn't being a little hard on the young man but she sensed that he was doing it deliberately.

David's eyes blazed as he sat up. 'Big deal! So I've managed two years without a fit. I suppose I should be grateful. But I don't feel grateful, believe me.' Suddenly all the fight seemed to drain out of him as he slumped against the pillows again. 'I wonder what Jessica is thinking. I bet she didn't bargain for a boyfriend who has fits!'

Claire had the feeling that they'd discovered the real reason for his anger. 'You haven't told her, I take it?'

David shook his head, groaning a little as it obviously made it throb. There was a gash on his left temple where a large bruise was forming and she guessed that it must be painful. 'No. It's hardly the best chat-up line in the world, is it? Hi, my name's David and I'm epileptic.'

She smiled in sympathy. 'I understand that. But it was probably a whole lot more scary for Jessica to have no idea what was happening. Maybe you should think about telling her.'

'And then I won't see her for dust!' David laughed wryly. 'Believe me, I *know* what her reaction will be—' He stopped abruptly. 'You haven't told her, have you?'

'No.' Sean moved back to the bed and examined the cut on his temple. 'It isn't hospital policy to discuss a patient with a third party. It's entirely up to you what you tell your friend. But if you want my advice, David, you'll tell her the truth because lying never does any good. However, what you must do is to go back to your own doctor. What have you been prescribed in the past to control the convulsions?'

'Carbamazepine, although I haven't taken it for about six months now,' David admitted.

'That could be a contributing factor as to why you

had an attack today. Also, you need to identify any other factors which might have acted as triggers, things like shortage of sleep or excess fluids. Both have been proved to set off an epileptic attack.'

'Jess and I were at a party all last night so we didn't get any sleep.' David frowned. 'Could that have caused it, do you think?'

'It's possible. My advice to you is to go back to your GP and discuss what happened with him. Epilepsy needn't ruin your life if you take control of it, David. That's all I'm saying. Now, I want you to stay here and rest for a while. Sister Shepherd will attend to that cut on your head. It isn't too deep so it won't need stitching.' He glanced at Claire and smiled. 'Over to you, Claire.'

Claire set about attending to the injury after Sean left. It didn't take long to clean up the gash and apply a few neat butterfly strips to hold it together. Covering it with a sterile dressing, she cleared everything away and started to leave.

'Do you think I should tell Jessica, Nurse?'

She paused and looked back, seeing the worry on David's face. Her heart ached for what he was going through because she understood it so well. Maybe their situations weren't the same but she knew what it felt like to be afraid to tell someone you cared for the truth.

'Only you can make that decision, David. But living with a lie isn't easy, I can tell you that.'

She gave him a last smile then hurried away, wishing with her whole heart that someone had given her that same piece of advice eight years ago. If she had known then how painful it would be, keeping the secret, would she have made the decision she'd made?

It was impossible to say, of course. Until Sean had

come back into her life she had been happy enough with what she had—Ben and a job she loved. Now she knew that she would never feel quite the same again. Having Sean back in her life, and realising what she might have had, changed things completely.

CHAPTER SEVEN

'COULD you come up to the office, please, Sister Shepherd?'

Claire frowned as she heard the request. She had been in the middle of dealing with a patient when she had been summoned to the phone. It was mid-afternoon and the department was still very busy. She was reluctant to leave when there was so much to do.

'Now? I have two nurses off sick today so we're pushed to our limit at the moment. Surely it can wait until I'm off duty?'

'I'm afraid not. Mr Hopkins was most insistent that he needed to see you immediately.'

'I see. Then I'll come up straight away.' Claire hung up, wondering why on earth she was being summoned to the manager's office. His secretary had made it sound urgent but she had no idea what he could want to see her about.

She went to find Margaret and tell her where she was going, shrugging as her friend demanded to know what was going on. 'I've no idea. All I was told was that I had to go up there immediately.'

'Sounds ominous to me.' Margaret glanced over Claire's shoulder and grimaced. 'What do you think it's all about, Sean? Claire has been summoned upstairs by the powers that be. What do you imagine they want?'

Claire looked round, feeling her heart jolt as she saw Sean coming along the corridor. That conversation she'd had with David Duggan earlier had unsettled her. Now she felt guiltier than ever as Sean came to join them, as though her secret were weighing even more heavily on her shoulders.

She saw Sean cast her a frowning glance and looked away, not needing to see the puzzlement in his eyes to tell her that he had sensed her nervousness. However, his tone was bland enough as he replied to Margaret's question.

'I've no idea, but I guessed there was something going on. They called Mike upstairs when you two were busy patching up that boy who came off his motorbike. I don't know what happened but Mike's been very uptight since then.'

'I suppose I'd better get up there and see what it's all about.' Claire summoned a smile, still carefully avoiding his eyes. 'If I'm not back by sundown send out the cavalry, guys!'

'Will do,' Margaret replied cheerfully as she hurried off to deal with a child who was about to be sick in Reception. Claire started towards the lifts, only to come to a halt as Sean caught her arm.

'What's wrong, Claire? I have this feeling that something is bothering you.'

'Nothing.' She gave a short laugh but it sounded strained even to her. 'Why on earth should you imagine anything is wrong, apart from the obvious such as being run off my feet all morning long and now being called up on high?'

Sean laughed, as she'd intended him to, but there was a searching quality to the look he gave her which made her heart skip a beat. 'Hmm, it's hardly been a bed of roses this morning, has it? But all that aside, I still have a feeling that something is worrying you.' His voice dropped so that nobody could overhear what he was saying. 'If you have a problem then I'd like to think you would come to me for help, Claire.'

She had to look away, afraid of what he would see in her eyes at that moment, all the heartache those softly spoken words set loose. 'Thank you, Sean. I…I appreciate that.'

'So you promise that if there's anything I can do, you'll ask me?' he urged.

She nodded, unable to push any words past the lump in her throat. He didn't try to detain her as she hurried away, and she was glad. His concern had been almost her undoing. It would have been only too easy to blurt out what was wrong, but it wasn't fair to appease her own guilty conscience that way. She had decided upon a course of action many years ago and there was no going back on it when it would disrupt so many lives.

Claire quickly made her way to the manager's office on the fourth floor. His secretary was at her desk and she looked up briefly from the report she was typing. 'Go straight in, Sister. They're waiting for you.'

They? Claire took a deep breath before entering the inner sanctum, not liking the sound of that at all, although she still had no idea what was going on. She looked around the room, taking note of the people present. Roger Hopkins, the hospital's manager, she knew from odd occasions when they'd met at social events organised by the hospital's League of Friends. She'd expected to see him there, of course, but she hadn't expected to be confronted by either Fiona Watts, the director of nursing, or Brian Haversham. There was another man there as well, whose face was vaguely familiar, although she couldn't recall where she had seen him before.

'Please, sit down, Sister Shepherd.' Roger Hopkins's

face was expressionless as he motioned her to a chair in front of the desk. He waited until Claire was seated before continuing. 'You already know Fiona and Brian, of course. But I don't think you've been introduced to the hospital trust's solicitor, Ian Runshaw.'

'Not introduced as such. However, Sister Shepherd and I have met—also in rather unfortunate circumstances,' Runshaw piped up.

It was his voice that jogged Claire's memory at last. Runshaw was the man who had made such a fuss that day about the length of time he'd had to wait. Was that what this was all about? she wondered. It wouldn't be the first time a patient had made a complaint, although she was certain that he had no grounds for making one now.

She gave him a cool nod, making no attempt to rise to the challenge. If Mr Runshaw had a grievance then let him come out with it. Anyone with an ounce of sense would soon see how petty he was being. However, it wasn't Mr Runshaw who picked up the conversation at that point but Brian Haversham.

'It has been brought to our attention that an incident occurred in A and E which may have resulted in the death of a patient, an incident which it appears you may be responsible for, Sister.'

'I beg your pardon?' Claire froze. She stared at Brian, seeing the dislike in his pale blue eyes. 'I have no idea what you are referring to, sir.'

'No? Then let me jog your memory. The man's name was Finch, Harold Finch. He was admitted suffering from severe chest pains brought on by an attack of angina. I assume you remember the case in question?'

'Of course. Mr Finch suffered a massive myocardial infarction while he was in A and E. Unfortunately, it wasn't possible to resuscitate him,' Claire answered quietly, although her own heart was beginning to race as she guessed where the conversation was leading.

'Maybe the resuscitation attempts would have had a better chance of succeeding if there had been more warning, Sister?' Brian smiled but there was no trace of warmth on his face. 'However, it appears that there was no warning because Mr Finch's monitor hadn't been set up correctly.'

Claire said nothing, mainly because she wasn't sure what to say in the circumstances. She was certain in her own mind that she had set up the equipment properly but she had no way of proving it.

'Nothing to say in your own defence, Sister Shepherd? Is that because you know that you made a grave error that day?' Mr Runshaw demanded.

Claire felt a rush of anger as she turned to him, making no attempt to conceal her dislike. 'I didn't make any error. The machine was working perfectly when I left Mr Finch. I'm quite certain of that.'

'Then how do you explain the fact that several of the electrodes weren't attached correctly when Mr Finch was discovered? One of your colleagues has just admitted that to us so there's no point in denying it.' Mr Runshaw gave her a chilly smile. 'I know how chaotic things were in the department that day. It seems to me that this was just another example of the lax attitude which seems to prevail there. Unfortunately, this error of yours could end up costing the hospital a great deal of money.'

'I don't understand.' Claire turned to Roger Hopkins for an explanation. She was reeling from the accusation and the unfair way in which she was being found guilty, without anyone bothering to listen to what she was saying. Roger was known as a fair-minded man so surely he wasn't going to jump on the bandwagon and prejudge her the way the others were doing? If he would just explain what was going on then listen to what she had to say, surely they could clear this up? However, his expression was less than encouraging.

'It appears that Mr Finch's family isn't happy about the treatment he received here. His son has instructed their solicitor to bring charges for negligence against this hospital. In the light of what has been revealed concerning the mistake over the monitoring system, it would appear he has a very strong case.'

He glanced down at his desk before he looked at Claire again. 'I'm afraid that I have no choice but to suspend you from duty, Sister Shepherd, until this situation has been resolved.'

'Suspend me! But it wasn't my fault, I tell you,' Claire cried in dismay. 'I am absolutely certain that everything was working properly when I left Mr Finch.'

'Unfortunately, that's going to be almost impossible to prove. In the meantime, the hospital cannot be seen to be employing a member of staff who made such a grave error.' Roger stood up, effectively putting an end to the meeting.

Claire left the office in a daze. Fiona Watts followed her out to explain what would happen next and advise her that it might be better if she got in touch with her union. Fiona seemed upset by what was happening but Claire barely heard her reassurances that she was sure this would all prove to be some sort of silly mistake.

Claire thanked her numbly then made her way back to A and E, wondering *how* she was going to prove that and clear her name…

'Claire? What is it? What's happened?'

She turned to Sean in despair as he came hurrying over to her, unaware that her face was paper white and that she was trembling from head to toe. 'I've been suspended from duty.'

'What?' He sounded as stunned as she felt. When he took her arm and quickly led her to the staffroom she made no protest. There was nobody in there as there hadn't been time for breaks that day. She walked blindly to the centre of the room as Sean closed the door to afford them some privacy, and just stood there, too dazed by what had happened to know what to do next.

'Come on, sweetheart, tell me what happened.' Sean's voice was soft as he coaxed her to tell him what had gone on. Claire felt a little warmth run through her as she heard the genuine concern it held.

She summoned a smile but it was a poor effort at best. 'Remember Mr Finch, the man with angina who died?'

'Yes.' Sean sounded puzzled. He leaned against the door with his arms folded as he studied her. Claire looked away, not proof against the concern she could see in his eyes. It would serve no purpose, giving in to the panic she could feel building inside her, but it was an effort to keep control.

She took a quick breath and forced herself to recount what had gone on. 'It seems his family isn't happy about the treatment he received here. They have instructed their solicitor to look into what happened. And…and somehow it came to light that Mr Finch's monitor wasn't working.'

'So they're laying the blame at your door?' Sean straightened abruptly. His face was grim as he came over to her. 'You told them that you'd set everything up correctly, I hope?'

'Of course I did! But it's my word against all the

evidence. I have no way of proving that I wasn't to blame,' she replied, feeling her panic rising another notch up the scale.

'I can't believe this! You're a damn fine nurse, Claire. You simply wouldn't make a mistake like that, no matter what evidence they think they have to the contrary.'

His vehemence made her smile, despite everything. 'Thank you. I'm grateful for your belief in me, Sean.'

'You don't need to be grateful!' He caught her by the shoulders and gave her a gentle shake. 'I know you, Claire. I know how you think, how you behave, how you feel...' He stopped as the full import of what he'd said hit him. His voice seemed to drop to new depths all of a sudden, the rich tone making a shudder pass through her body, as she heard it.

'I know you, Claire, as well as I know myself.' His hands slid down her arms, gently kneading the soft flesh, leaving behind a lingering feeling of warmth and comfort. 'I know that you are incapable of lying about something so important.'

It was just too much to hear him say that. Claire was overcome with shame. How would he feel if he found out about the lies she'd told about Ben? Would Sean still believe that he knew her so well then?

She moved away so that his hands fell from her arms, chilled to her soul by the thought of his belief in her being shaken to its very foundations. 'Maybe you don't know me as well as you think you do, Sean,' she whispered hollowly.

'What do you mean by that?' he asked at once, his brows drawing into a heavy frown.

She shook her head, sick to her stomach with worry and guilt. 'Nothing. It's just been a shock, that's all,' she replied dully.

'It must have been. What are you going to do about it, though, Claire? You aren't going to let them get away with this ridiculous accusation, surely?'

His anger was evident in the harsh bite of his voice, and she shrugged. 'I'm not sure yet. I'll have to think about it, see if I can come up with any ideas as to how I can convince them that I wasn't at fault. In the meantime, I've been suspended while they make their enquiries. I suppose I'd better get myself off home.'

'That's probably the best thing to do at present. I'll find out what's going on and see if I can't talk some sense into them.' His tone was grim and she gave him a watery little smile as she collected her bag from her locker. Sean didn't say anything else before she left. She was glad. Now she was more certain than ever that revealing what she had done would destroy everything he had ever felt for her.

If Sean discovered how she had lied to him he would never be able to believe in her again...and she couldn't bear that on top of everything else that had happened!

It was gone ten when there was a knock on the door that night. Claire hurried to answer it, not wanting Ben to be disturbed. She had skirted round the reason she had been home when Ben had got in from school by telling him that she had a few days' leave still to take. He was a sensitive child and she hadn't wanted him worrying about what had happened.

He had accepted her explanation readily enough but, then, he had no reason to think she was lying. To Ben's mind she always told the truth, and realising that simply increased her sense of guilt.

'Hello, Claire. I hope you don't mind me calling round so late but I wanted to see how you were.'

It was a shock to open the door and find Sean on the step. Claire took a quick breath, struggling to get a grip on herself. 'I…I'm OK,' she managed at last, before realising that she couldn't leave him standing outside. 'Come in.'

'If you're sure I'm not disturbing you…' He hesitated only a moment before stepping into the hall, waiting while she closed the door before continuing quietly, 'I'm afraid it isn't really good news, Claire, so, please, don't get your hopes up that's why I'm here.'

She gave a small shrug. 'I never thought it would be. Anyway, let's go into the sitting-room while we talk. Ben's in bed and I don't want him being woken up.'

She led the way and sat down on a chair while Sean sat on the settee. Now that she had a chance to look at him properly she could see how tired he was.

'You look worn out,' she said in concern. 'You shouldn't be here at this time of the night, worrying about me and my problems.'

'I wouldn't have been able to rest if I hadn't seen you. I just wanted to check how you were. I could tell how upset you were when you left work, and no wonder.' He ran his hand through his hair and sighed wearily. 'I stayed on to do an extra shift—Lee Aspinall went off sick so they were stuck. It was better than going home and sitting there, worrying about what's happened.'

'It isn't your problem, Sean,' she assured him quickly. 'It's mine.'

He shook his head decisively. 'No, that's where you're wrong. I've made it clear both to Roger Hopkins and Brian Haversham that I take full responsibility for what went on. Harold Finch was my patient, Claire, and I was responsible for him at the end of the day.'

'But that isn't fair! You know it isn't, Sean.' She

stood up abruptly, both deeply touched and worried about him trying to protect her by taking the blame. 'I was responsible for setting up the monitoring equipment. You know that as well as I do.'

She held up her hand when he went to interrupt, her brown eyes blazing at him. 'You know I'm right!'

He frowned heavily. 'Damn it, Claire, I only want to help! I just can't stand aside and let them treat you like this. What is it with this Haversham guy, anyway? He seems to have a real downer on you.'

She gave a shaky laugh, not sure whether she had managed to convince him that this was her problem and not his. 'I'm afraid Brian Haversham and I got off on the wrong foot when I first arrived here. He made rather a nuisance of himself at the Christmas party and didn't appreciate it when I let him know that I wasn't interested. He's been waiting his chance to pay me back ever since.'

Sean's mouth compressed and he looked so grim that her heart turned over. 'I should have realised there was something personal behind this! It has the feel of some sort of vendetta. Well, if he thinks he can get away with it he can think again…'

'Please, don't do anything that might get you into trouble, Sean!' she pleaded. 'I know Haversham. He's a nasty piece of work and now that he has that solicitor, Runshaw, to back him up, heaven knows what he'll try.'

'Runshaw was there when I went up to see Hopkins. I recognised him immediately.' Sean laughed softly. 'He recognised me as well from the speed with which he left. Anyway, I made sure that Hopkins knew what had gone on that day in A and E, when Runshaw molested you. He didn't say much but I could tell that he took note of it. He seems a decent sort of a chap, so I'm fairly confident that he'll listen to any evidence we can come up with to prove your innocence.'

Claire sighed. 'What evidence, though? That's the problem. I can't *prove* that I connected up that machine correctly because nobody saw me doing it...' She paused.

'What is it, sweetheart? What have you thought of?' he demanded eagerly.

Her heart turned over at the use of that gentle endearment even while she told herself that it meant nothing. She rushed on, anxious to quell the warm little glow which had settled in a cold dark corner of her heart. 'Remember that old lady who was sharing the room with Mr Finch... Mrs Dennis, wasn't it?'

'The lady with the broken hip?' Sean gave a whoop of delight as he shot to his feet and grabbed hold of her hands. 'You think she may have seen something to explain the mystery? Is that it?'

'I don't know. I...I remember passing one of the theatre staff, with her pre-med as I was leaving the room,' she said shakily, trying to ignore the sensations that were flowing through her fingertips. 'Mrs Dennis might not have noticed anything once she'd taken it.'

'But it's worth a try! Come on, Claire, admit it—it's the best lead we have.' He suddenly drew her to him and hugged her. Relief had deepened his voice so that it seemed to rumble beneath her ear. 'Please, heaven, she did see something!'

Claire tried to say something but words were beyond her right then. The feel of Sean's strong body next to hers was setting up a chain of reactions the like of which she couldn't recall having felt before. There was a deep sense of comfort at being held like this after all the worry the day had brought, but mixed in with it were other feelings, far more fiery and demanding…

She wasn't sure whether it was the way she tensed that alerted him. It was impossible not to react, of course, when her body was responding of its own accord to his closeness. Yet suddenly Sean eased her away from him and looked deep into her eyes with an expression in his own which made her heart race. What she could see in his eyes was everything she was feeling and it shook her to the core to see the evidence of it.

'Sean…' She wasn't even aware of saying his name, let alone of reaching up to lay her hand against his cheek so that she could feel the warmth of his skin beneath her palm. She felt him take a deep breath before he drew her to him once more and enfolded her in his arms as though that was the one place on earth she was meant to be.

Maybe it was, she thought giddily. Hadn't there always been something missing from her life since he'd gone out of it, a gap which not even Ben had been able to fill? Yet, feeling Sean's strong arms around her, suddenly she felt whole again.

The thought barely had time to form when he bent and kissed her, gently, tenderly, but with an aching need that awoke an answering need in her. There was no time to wonder if it was right or wrong to feel this way, to work out whether or not it was foolish or sane. Sean kissed her and she kissed him back—it was as simple and uncomplicated as that.

Her lips parted instinctively, slipping easily into just the right shape to accommodate his, knowing exactly what to do. It was as though the years apart had never happened and they were the same two people they had always been. When his tongue slid between her lips to tangle with hers she gave a soft little moan, winding her arms tighter around his neck, holding him just as close as he was holding her. It felt so good to have him this close again, so right…

He let her go so abruptly that she staggered, but he made no attempt to steady her. She had the feeling that he didn't trust himself to reach out and touch her because he wasn't sure what might happen… But maybe that was just her being fanciful, she realised coldly, because there was little evidence of it in the flat, controlled tone of his voice.

'I'm sorry, Claire. That was incredibly crass of me. All I can do is apologise and say that I never meant to take advantage of you in any way.'

'Advantage?' she repeated through lips which felt numb all of a sudden.

'Yes! This whole unpleasant episode with Finch has been a dreadful shock for you and you must be feeling very mixed up about what's happened. It's no wonder that you don't know whether you're on your head or your heels at the moment.'

She knew what he was saying, of course, that it had been the stress of what had happened that day which had prompted her response. She bit her lip to hold back a slightly hysterical laugh.

Did Sean really believe that? Maybe. But what would he say if she told him that it had had nothing to do with it, that she had wanted his kiss for itself and no other reason? Would he be pleased, sorry, shocked? Would he then admit that it hadn't been just a need to comfort her which had prompted him to take her in his arms in the first place? Would…would it really be wise to say any of those things when it could be setting them on course to disaster? How could she encourage any sort of relationship between them when it could only result in Ben getting hurt?

It was that last thought which gave her the strength to know what to do. No matter what it cost her personally, she would never do anything to hurt her son!

'Please, don't apologise, Sean,' she said flatly, barely able to push the words past the lump in her throat. 'I…I think we both got a bit carried away in the heat of the moment.'

'I'm sure you're right.' There was no inflection in his voice now and little expression on his face as she glanced at him. He seemed to have accepted her explanation readily enough but maybe that was because he wanted to accept it. Sean had made it plain from the outset that all he was aiming for was to renew their friendship, nothing else. He must be as keen as she was to avoid any complications, although for a different reason!

She saw him to the door, tensing as he paused on the step, and she was suddenly reminded of what had happened the last time. She didn't think she could bear it if he kissed her again, no matter if it *was* just a social token!

However, he was all business as he turned to her. 'I'll see what I can find out from Mrs Dennis, Claire. It might take me a few days as I'm on duty until the weekend, so just bear with me.'

'Maybe I could go and see her myself?' she suggested, trying to follow his lead and confine her thoughts to the problem at hand. It shouldn't have been difficult because it was such a huge problem, but it was hard to concentrate as her mind kept returning to those moments in Sean's arms when he'd kissed her and held her as though he'd really wanted it to happen…

'No, that wouldn't be a good idea.' His tone was curt enough to focus her full attention on what was happening, although it wavered momentarily as she saw the glitter which lit his eyes...

'Why not?' she asked quickly, refusing to allow herself to wonder about it.

'Because we daren't give them grounds for saying that you coerced Mrs Dennis into lying for you. If she *did* see anything then we have to convince everyone—Haversham and Runshaw included—that her statement is true.' His mouth thinned. 'We simply can't risk any slip-ups, Claire. That pair are out to get you, albeit for two entirely different reasons!'

She shivered at that. 'It's horrible to know that anyone would go to such lengths to destroy my reputation.'

He touched her hand lightly. 'It is. But they aren't going to win, Claire. I promise you that!'

He left straight after that, striding quickly down the path to his car. Claire closed the door as he drove away. She leaned against it, feeling unutterably weary.

Would Sean find the evidence they needed? Her life would be in ruins if he didn't. If the hospital dismissed her on the grounds of professional imcompetence, it would be impossible to find employment anywhere else. Yet as she stood there it wasn't the only thought that troubled her. There were so many other things on her mind as well...

CHAPTER EIGHT

THE next week passed in a blur as Claire struggled to keep a grip on the panic that assailed her constantly. She got in touch with her union representative and set up a time for a meeting with the union's solicitor, but it all seemed vaguely unreal, as though it were happening to somebody else, not her.

When she received a letter from the hospital board, formally suspending her and setting out the terms for a hearing, she came close to despair. It was only the need to protect Ben that kept her carrying on as normal, but as each day passed and she heard nothing from Sean her fears grew. If she couldn't prove her innocence then what would she do?

Margaret and several others from the hospital rang to offer their support, for which she was grateful. She didn't tell them about Mrs Dennis because it was such a slim hope that the old lady might have seen something that she hardly dared cling to it. She had to put her trust in Sean and hope that he would be able to find out the truth somehow.

In an effort to take her mind off all the worry, she took Ben to the cinema on the Friday night, hoping to lose herself in the adventure film they saw, but it didn't work. She just sat, staring at the screen, while her mind ran riot. They stopped off for a burger on the way home, Ben chattering excitedly about the film they'd seen. He was blissfully unaware of Claire's distraction, thankfully. She didn't want him worrying as well.

It was almost ten when they arrived home to find Sean parked outside. He got out of his car as they drew up, smiling as Ben gave a great whoop of delight when he saw him.

'Sean! Wow, this is brill! I wish you'd come earlier then you could have come to the cinema with us, couldn't he, Mum?'

'Er, yes.' Claire summoned a smile for the child's benefit as she handed him the front door key. 'You go and put the kettle on while Sean locks his car, darling. You will come in for a cup of coffee, won't you?' she asked as an afterthought as Ben hurried away. After what had gone on the other night she could hardly blame him if he didn't want to spend too much time with her.

'I'm not sure that coffee is the best idea,' he said, his face completely deadpan so that her heart sank. The thought that she might have lost Sean's support was almost more than she could bear.

She was just trying to come to terms with the idea when he reached into the car and lifted out a tissue-wrapped bottle. 'This might be more the order of the day.'

Claire took it from him and peeled away the paper, her heart beginning to hammer as she saw the label on the bottle. 'Champagne? But why—?'

She got no further as Sean suddenly lifted her off her feet and swung her around. 'Why do you think? Mrs Dennis remembers quite clearly what happened that day—Harold Finch unhooked the electrodes himself *and* unplugged the machine!'

'He did? And she's sure of that?' She couldn't seem to take in what he was telling her. She took a deep breath as sheer relief made her go weak. 'You're sure?'

'One hundred per cent positive, my sweet!' he assured

her with such conviction that her doubts faded completely. He set her down on her feet and looped his arm around her waist, obviously realising that she needed a bit of support to make it up the path.

'Come on, I'll tell you the whole story once you're sitting down. I'd hate you to drop that very expensive bottle of bubbly!

Claire laughed shakily as she let him lead her inside. Ben popped his head round the kitchen door as he heard them. 'Can I have hot chocolate, Mum? And can I make it myself?'

The practicalities steadied her a bit. 'Yes, so long as you're very careful with that boiling water,' she warned.

'Course!' Ben assured her in a voice that spoke volumes about mothers who fussed. He looked at the bottle she was holding and, with a maturity which made her smile, said, 'Do you and Sean still want coffee if you've got that wine?'

Sean answered for her. 'I think we'll give it a miss, thanks, Ben. We just need a couple of glasses if you can find them for us.'

'Sure.' Ben disappeared and came back a few seconds later with two tumblers, cheerily decorated with cartoon characters. Sean took them without blinking, as though drinking expensive champagne out of glasses like that was the only way to do it.

'Thanks. Look, if you don't mind, Ben, your mum and I have something we need to talk about, work stuff, you understand?' he explained to the boy.

Ben nodded understandingly. 'That's OK. I'll go upstairs and read. But you will come again soon, Sean? You did promise that we could play another game of football so that you could try to even the score!'

Sean groaned comically. 'I'd love to come again, Ben,

although I don't know if my legs can take another game of football!'

Ben laughed as he went to make his chocolate, before going to bed. Claire smiled as he disappeared. 'He sounded so grown-up just now, didn't he?' She glanced at the glasses Sean was holding and grimaced. 'Although it's obvious that his education is sorely lacking in some areas! We haven't had many occasions to drink champagne, as you probably gathered.'

'I don't think it makes any difference what sort of glasses we drink from. This wine is going to taste fantastic because of the reason we're drinking it!' he assured her, stepping aside for her to lead the way into the sitting-room.

He waited while she had switched on some lights then popped the cork and half filled the tumblers. 'Here's to your good name being restored, Claire,' he said handing her one of the glasses and raising the other aloft in a toast.

'Amen to that!' she replied wholeheartedly, chinking her glass against his before sitting down. 'So, come on, tell me exactly what you found out.'

'Well, first of all I want to apologize for not getting in touch all week, but I've been working virtually double shifts every day, with Lee still being off sick. It wasn't until this morning that I managed to visit Mrs Dennis.' He paused to sip some of his wine and Claire made herself wait patiently for him to continue.

'Anyway, the matron at the nursing home was delighted to see me. It turns out that Mrs Dennis has been going on and on about what she saw, only they thought she must have been imagining it. I spoke to the old lady and she told me that she had seen Harold Finch get up and start undoing the electrodes and pull the plug out of the socket. Evidently, she'd had her pre-med but she was certain of what she saw.'

'Why didn't she say something to the theatre staff when they came to collect her?' Claire asked, frowning.

'She said that she tried to tell them but the medication must have been taking effect by then and they didn't understand what she was saying. Evidently, Finch had lain down on the bed again by the time they arrived to take her upstairs.'

Sean shrugged. 'Whether he wasn't feeling too good or he was trying to avoid anyone noticing what he was up to, we'll never know. You know as well as I do how reluctant he was to remain in hospital so it might very well have been the latter.'

'The silly man!' Claire exclaimed. 'Putting his life at risk that way...' She sighed. 'Didn't Mrs Dennis mention what she had seen to the staff on the ward once she came round from her operation?'

'No. She said that at first she thought she must have been dreaming and then she was worried in case people thought her mind was going. She kept it to herself until she got back to the nursing home but then it started to prey on her mind. The matron told me that they were wondering if they should contact us as Mrs Dennis was getting so distressed. I told her briefly what had happened and she immediately offered to ring Roger Hopkins and tell him all she knew.'

Sean smiled. 'The fact that Mrs Dennis had told everyone at the nursing home what she had seen *before* I spoke to her simply strengthened our case. Hopkins went to visit Mrs Dennis this afternoon. Apparently, he has instructed Runshaw to take a full statement from the old lady, which will be passed to Harold Finch's solicitors in the morning.'

'So, does that mean that I'm in the clear even though I forgot to tell the chauffeur that Finch wanted to see him?' Claire asked, unable to believe that it could end so quickly.

'They simply don't have a case against you now, sweetheart. In fact, you could sue them for defamation of character if you chose to,' Sean explained gently.

She shook her head so that the heavy weight of her hair swirled around her shoulders. She hadn't bothered pinning it up that day, but had simply tied it back with a black ribbon. It hung halfway down her back, gleaming richly red in the light from a nearby lamp. 'I don't want to do that. All I want is my name cleared so that I can go back to work.'

'I'm sure they will be more than pleased to hear that, Claire.' Sean's tone was flat all of a sudden. When she shot him a curious look she could see that he was staring down at his glass...

She wouldn't allow herself to wonder what was wrong with him, she told herself sternly, although her heart was beating crazily as she sensed a sudden shift in his mood. 'Then all I can say is thank you, Sean. Thank you from the bottom of my heart for all the trouble you've been to on my behalf.'

His eyes lifted to her face and he smiled at her with such tenderness that her breath caught. 'It was my pleasure, Claire,' he said softly, with aching sincerity. 'All I ever wanted was to look after you.'

She wasn't sure what to say. Anything seemed too much or too little at that moment. She just looked at him and saw the truth in the depths of his eyes and it both thrilled her and scared her.

Sean still cared about her! She wouldn't let her mind go any further, wouldn't let it admit the word she both longed to hear and yet dreaded. It was enough to know that he cared and far too much to think that he might still *love* her.

He raised his glass, his eyes still holding hers fast. 'To you, Claire. No matter what has happened, I shall always be glad we met.'

She lifted her glass to her lips but it was impossible to swallow even a drop of the wine. When Sean rose to his feet she remained where she was because she was afraid that her legs wouldn't hold her if she tried to stand. He set his glass on the coffee-table then gave her a brief smile, and she was glad that his gaze was hooded now. It would have been too much to see that same expression in his eyes a second time and not respond to it.

'I'd better go. If you need me you know where I am, Claire.'

'Th-thank you, Sean. For everything,' she whispered, struggling to hold back the tears.

She saw his shoulders rise and fall in a gesture that spoke of regret and acceptance. 'I haven't done anything, Claire. Nothing you need thank me for, anyway. I most certainly didn't do what I should have done all those years ago.'

He didn't explain but, then, he didn't need to. Sean blamed himself for their break-up, putting it down to his need to work overseas.

She got up unsteadily as he left the house and switched on the television, turning the volume up so that she couldn't hear him driving away. She didn't need to be reminded that she couldn't ask him to stay. It was too dangerous to do that. Sean had to leave because there wasn't any choice. He couldn't stay and remain in ignorance of the fact that he was Ben's father. He couldn't be told because Ben would suffer. It was a cleft-stick situation and she was right in the middle of it, unable to turn one way or the other without someone getting hurt.

'It's good to have you back, Claire!' Margaret glanced round the table. 'We all knew you weren't to blame for what happened, didn't we, folks?'

There was a chorus of agreement and Claire smiled her thanks. It was lunchtime on her first day back and they were all gathered in the staff canteen to celebrate her reinstatement with cottage pie and strong cups of tea. It was such a contrast to how she and Sean had celebrated the news a few days earlier that she couldn't help but think about the difference.

She sighed as she picked up her cup while the conversation turned to more general topics. She hadn't seen Sean alone since the night he'd called round to tell her the good news. She'd seen him in work that morning, of course, but they had both been too busy to stop and chat, although she couldn't help thinking that he might have managed to find the odd moment if he'd wanted to.

Was Sean avoiding her? she found herself wondering. There had been a certain reserve about the way he'd greeted her that morning, unless it was just her being overly sensitive in view of what had happened the other night, of course. Wondering if Sean still loved her, that was bound to put her on edge!

'Claire, have you got a minute?'

She looked round as someone tapped her on the shoulder, smiling as she saw that it was Mike Kennedy. He was in his street clothes and she wondered what he was doing at work when he wasn't on duty until that evening.

'Of course. What is it?' she asked, getting up when

he motioned for her to follow him. They went out onto the terrace and Mike shut the door so that no one could overhear what they said.

'I owe you an apology, Claire,' he said, sounding very ill at ease. 'It's all my fault that this trouble started you see. All I can say is that I never meant it to happen.'

She frowned, not sure what he was trying to say. 'I'm not with you, Mike. How can it be your fault?'

'Because I happened to mention to someone about Finch's monitor not being set up, and Brian Haversham overheard me.' His pleasant face darkened into a frown. 'When Finch's family kicked up a fuss Haversham hauled me into his office and demanded to know what had gone on. I had to tell him, Claire, because there simply wasn't any way to avoid it.'

'It wasn't your fault, Mike. And I don't want you blaming yourself either,' Claire assured him quickly. 'Haversham has been waiting for his chance to get back at me and I suppose he saw this as the perfect opportunity.'

'But if I'd just kept my big mouth shut!' He let out a huge sigh. 'I wasn't accusing you of not setting it up correctly, you understand, Claire. I was simply trying to work out how it came to be unplugged.'

'And now we know how—Finch did it himself.' She laid her hand on his arm, hating to see how upset he was. 'It's all over and done with, Mike…really.'

'Thanks, Claire. It's a great weight off my mind, I can tell you! I just had to come in today to see you and get things straight.'

He gave her a quick hug, buzzing her cheek with a friendly kiss which stemmed more from relief at being exonerated than anything else. Mike was in a stable relationship himself and his interest in her was zero in that respect, as she knew very well. However, as he hurried away, Claire realised that they had attracted an audience.

Her heart leapt as she saw Sean standing by the window. He had obviously seen what had gone on because there was the oddest expression on his face…

He swung round abruptly so that by the time she went back into the canteen he was nowhere to be seen. Claire sat down at the table to finish her lunch but the food tasted like sawdust. She kept thinking about what she had seen on Sean's face just now. Jealousy? Was it possible?

Her hand shook as she lifted the cooling tea to her lips. Even if she was right, there was little she could do about it. She could hardly go to him and explain that she wasn't interested in anyone else because she still cared for him!

'Claire, can you come with me, please?'

She looked round but Sean was already heading back to the cubicles. She had just come back from lunch and hadn't had a chance to acquaint herself with any new admissions which had come in during her break.

She glanced at the board where the patients' names were written and gasped as she spotted one familiar one—Helen Morris, the lady who had been brought in a couple of weeks earlier with heart block.

She hurried to the cubicle and found Sean checking the electrocardiograph. He looked round as he heard her footsteps, although his face betrayed nothing other than professional concern. Claire found herself wondering if she had imagined that brief display of emotion she'd witnessed earlier.

'Mrs Morris has had a recurrence of the problem,' he explained quietly as he moved to the foot of the bed.

'She blacked out in the street while out shopping and the monitor is showing an abnormally slow heartbeat.'

'Shall I ring for Brian Haversham?' Claire offered, although her own heart sank at the thought of having to face the senior registrar so soon after her reinstatement. Brian was certainly not going to be pleased by what had happened, she suspected.

'I've already done that. He'll be down as soon as he's free. In the meantime, Claire, I'd like you to see if you can get Mrs Morris to tell you everything she did this morning, leading up to when she blacked out.' Sean frowned.

'There's something odd about all this which doesn't fit the usual pattern. With normal heart block the patient experiences a range of symptoms—fatigue, breathlessness, often swelling of the legs. Mrs Morris is quite emphatic that she hasn't suffered any of those things. Added to which, when she was in for observation the last time, there was no sign of any problem. Once the drugs had taken effect her heartbeat returned to normal.'

'How strange. Did the herbalist contact you last time about those tablets she was taking, by the way?' Claire queried, taking her lead from him and keeping her tone brisk.

'Yes. He was adamant that they couldn't have caused the trouble. And his view was backed up by the lab report. However, there was something rather surprising which turned up in the blood tests. Take a look.' He passed her a slip of paper from Mrs Morris's file.

Claire read it quickly, gasping as she came to the part he meant. 'Traces of digitalis? But Mrs Morris hasn't been treated with any drugs of that type to the best of our knowledge.'

'No, she hasn't. As her husband told us, she's reluctant to see her doctor and any of the digitalis drugs need to be prescribed as they're extremely toxic.' Sean frowned heavily. 'I even checked back with the lab just to make sure that the test results were from blood taken before Mrs Morris was treated by us. Neither I nor Haversham prescribed any of the digitalis drugs to sort out her problem last time, but I just wanted to make certain that no one had made a mistake.'

Claire sighed. 'It's always best to cover all the bases, isn't it?'

Sean smiled grimly. 'That was my opinion, too. However, the lab is positive that the results we have here are from blood taken before Mrs Morris received any treatment from us. Evidently, they enter the time and the date when they receive samples for testing...see, right there.'

He pointed to the top right-hand corner of the slip. Claire nodded as she saw the time and date neatly typed in the appropriate space.

'So where did she get the digitalis from?' she queried, then gasped. 'You think it's something she's taken herself, one of those remedies she makes?'

'Exactly.' He grinned at her, his whole face lighting up all of a sudden. 'That's why I find it so good working with you, Claire. We're on the same wavelength!'

She felt a small stab of pain on hearing him say that. It wouldn't do any good to dwell on it, she told herself sternly, but she glimpsed something in Sean's eyes which told her that he was just as aware of what he had said as she was.

'Anyway, see what you can get out of her, will you, Claire? She's a bit groggy but she seems to know what's going on.' He was businesslike once more as he pushed back the curtain. 'I'll check back with you after I've taken another look at the child in cubicle six.'

Claire sighed as he left, realising that she shouldn't resent the way he seemed able to separate his thoughts into two neat compartments. Work had to come first for both of them, but it was hard for her to make the division between professional and personal feelings.

She drew up a chair beside the bed. 'Hello, Mrs Morris. I can't say this is a pleasure, seeing you here again. I was hoping that we'd sorted you out the last time!'

Helen gave a shaky laugh. 'Can't say that I want to be back here either. It was awful, Sister. I just felt this horrible blackness welling up…'

Tears filled her eyes and Claire patted her hand. 'It must have been really scary for you. That's why we want to find out what's making you ill. Your husband told us the last time you were here that you make a lot of home remedies for any minor ailments you have—is that right?'

'Oh, yes. My boys call them my witch's brews.' Helen managed to smile before she sobered abruptly. 'You think it might be something I've made which is causing this? But I'm so careful!'

'I'm sure you are. And it could turn out that we are on entirely the wrong track. However, can you tell me if you've taken anything recently that you've prepared yourself?' Claire asked soothingly.

'Well, I made myself a tisane of comfrey leaves this morning,' Helen said slowly. 'That's a sort of herb tea. I've been having a bit of tummy trouble lately and my granny always swore by it, said that it did her a power of good. I usually find it helps because it's so rich in minerals and vitamins.'

'So it isn't something new?' Claire queried. 'You've made this…tisane before?'

'Oh, yes, lots of times. Although I've had a bit of trouble finding the plant recently. The place where I usually gather the leaves has been fenced off for some sort of development project so I've had to go elsewhere. I was so pleased when I came across it while I was out walking the dog a few weeks back. I went back there this morning and collected some fresh leaves then made myself a cup of the tea as soon as I got home. I didn't drink it all, though, because it tasted so bitter. I noticed that the last time, funnily enough.'

'I see. And you've not taken anything else?' Claire sighed when Helen shook her head. 'Well, I'll get onto the herbalist in town and see what he has to say about this comfrey, but it doesn't appear that it could be the cause of your problem, does it? In the meantime, you try to rest until Mr Haversham is free to see you.'

Helen shut her eyes as Claire quietly left the cubicle. She went straight to the phone and rang the shop, and was relieved when the herbalist answered. She quickly outlined the problem they had and felt a little rush of excitement when the man gasped.

'You say that Mrs Morris mentioned the tisane tasted very bitter?'

'Yes, that's right. Evidently, she didn't finish the drink because of the taste. Does that mean something?' she queried.

'It could do. To be frank, not many people drink comfrey tea nowadays, although it's marvellous for intestinal problems and things like diarrhoea. Mostly it's used as a poultice for healing cuts and bruises or for reducing swelling.

'However, you need to be careful when collecting any

leaves for medicinal purposes because it's easy to mistake one plant for another. What struck me immediately is that comfrey and foxglove leaves look very alike, especially when the plants are young. It sounds to me as though Mrs Morris may have mistaken one for the other, which would explain why she found the drink so bitter. It's well known that animals avoid foxgloves because of their bitter taste!' he explained.

'And the drug, digitalis, is derived from foxgloves, isn't it?' Claire said, delighted that they might have solved the mystery.

'That's right. The word "digitalis" is the Latin name for the foxglove plant so it certainly seems to fit, doesn't it? Would it help if I went round to her house and checked it out for you?' he offered immediately.

'Would you? That's really very kind.' Claire gave him her name and he promised to phone her back as soon as he could. She was just putting the phone back on its rest when Sean appeared. She quickly outlined what she had learned and he rolled his eyes in disbelief.

'I don't believe it! It does seem to fit, though. Digitalis drugs work by slowing down the heart rate, thus making each beat more effective in pumping the blood. However, they can make it stop beating altogether if the level of toxicity builds up, which is why patients taking digitalis need to be closely monitored. If it turns out that Mrs Morris has been making this tisane from foxglove leaves then it's little wonder she's been having problems!'

Claire laughed. 'Let's hope we're right! And I think we should try to persuade her to give up preparing these witch's brews, don't you?'

'Amen to that! We have enough patients as it is, without people trying to poison themselves.' His smile was warmly appreciative as he looked at her. 'Well done, Claire! I should have known you'd get to the bottom of this.'

'All part of the job,' she replied lightly, but she couldn't deny how good it felt to hear him say that. She gave him a quick smile then turned to hurry away.

She paused, however, as Sean said suddenly, 'What are you doing on Saturday?'

Her heart picked up its beat, even though she knew how foolish it was. It was an effort to keep all expressions from her face as she turned. 'I'm not sure yet. Housework undoubtedly, washing, ironing…'

'Please!' He held up his hands. 'You're making me feel tired just hearing you list all those dreadful boring chores!' He gave her an oddly hesitant smile. 'I was going to suggest that I take you and Ben out somewhere for the day if you weren't too busy. I could do with a break *and* it will be a perfect way to get out of playing that return game of football I promised him!'

'Well, I'm not sure…' she began, realising that it wouldn't be wise to accept the offer, no matter how much she wanted to.

'Please, don't say no!' He fixed a comically pleading expression to his face but it didn't disguise the intentness of the look he gave her. 'If you've made plans to spend the day with someone else then obviously you can't alter your arrangements. But if it's just the vacuuming that's stopping you, couldn't you leave it until another time? I'm sure your compassionate heart would hate to see a grown man weeping because he's been beaten by your son once again!'

Claire laughed, as she'd been meant to, but her heart was thudding strongly. In his own way, Sean was trying to find out if she had made plans to see another man, like Mike Kennedy, for instance. It went a long way to prove that she'd been right and that he had been jealous.

In the circumstances, the last thing she should have done was accept, but suddenly she found herself throwing caution to the winds. 'We'd love to come, Sean. Thanks.'

'Great.' He looked round as a flurry of movement announced Brian Haversham's arrival, and his tone became suddenly grim. 'We'll sort out the details later. OK?'

'Fine.' She watched him stride over to the senior registrar. The two men's body language spoke volumes about their feelings, she thought. It was obvious that Brian didn't like Sean and just as obvious how Sean felt! The thought that she might be the cause of their antagonism gave her a momentary qualm before she realised that it wasn't going to have any really disastrous repercussions. Sean would be leaving in a few weeks' time so whether or not he and Brian saw eye to eye was of little importance.

She hurried back to take another look at Helen Morris, trying to stave off the feeling of emptiness at the thought of how it was going to be when Sean had left. She would deal with that when it happened. For now she had the outing to look forward to because all of a sudden she really *was* looking forward to it. A whole day spent with Sean and Ben would give her so many wonderful memories to look back on.

CHAPTER NINE

SATURDAY dawned bright and clear. Claire was up before seven and had a picnic lunch all ready and packed before Ben came down for breakfast half an hour later.

'Scotch eggs and sausage rolls...*and* chicken! Wicked, Mum!' he exclaimed, rooting through the hamper.

'There's also a cherry cake and some early strawberries,' she told him, taking the plastic box out of the fridge and stowing it carefully into the hamper. The strawberries had been dreadfully expensive and had made a big dent in her housekeeping, but she'd felt like splashing out for once.

Ben sat down and began spooning up cornflakes at a great rate. 'What time is Sean coming?'

'Eight o'clock. He told me that he wanted to make an early start so that we could get the best out of the day,' she told the child for at least the tenth time. Ben had been absolutely thrilled at the prospect of a whole day out, making her guiltily aware of how rarely they enjoyed such a treat.

There was always so much to do, with the shopping and housework, that her days off tended to be swallowed up by chores. However, she promised herself that she would make more free time so that they could go out and enjoy themselves in the future, although, of course, this day was special because Sean was sharing it with them...

She closed the hamper lid then drank the rest of her

coffee, not allowing herself to think ahead to the time when Sean wouldn't be around. 'Right, kiddo, as soon as you've eaten your breakfast I want you to go upstairs and find your cagoule and a sweater in case it turns cold later. And don't forget to go to the loo—we might not be able to stop wherever we're going.'

'OK.' Ben bolted the rest of his cereal then raced out of the room. It was amazing, Claire thought, how one small boy could make as much noise as a herd of elephants!

Sean arrived on the dot of eight and Ben was down the path before he could get out of the car. 'Where are we going?' he demanded eagerly. 'Mum wouldn't tell me!'

'That's because your mum doesn't know. It's a surprise,' Sean explained, laughing at the child's excitement before his gaze moved to Claire as she came to join them.

'Hi,' he said softly, his blue eyes taking very thorough stock of what she was wearing. 'No need to ask how you are this morning, Claire. You look wonderful.'

'Oh...thank you.' She felt a wash of colour run up her cheeks as she saw the appreciation in his eyes. She had taken extra care with her appearance that day and it was nice to know that he had noticed.

Her pale blue denim jeans were freshly laundered and fitted snugly around her slim hips, while the crisp white blouse she had chosen to go with them looked both casual and elegant. A narrow tan leather belt around her waist and tan loafers on her feet completed her outfit, although she had both a sweater and a jacket in case they were needed later.

She had spent some time debating how to do her hair, considering her usual chignon too severe for a relaxed day out. In the end, she had French-plaited the thick curls, letting the tail of the plait hang between her shoulder blades. She had wondered if the style was a bit too young for her but her fears seemed groundless in view of Sean's obvious admiration.

She turned to Ben, realising all of a sudden that the silence was starting to run on a little too long. 'Right, have you got everything you need, then?'

'I think so… Oops, hang on a sec!' He shot off into the house and Sean laughed softly.

'He's like a miniature dynamo! How do you manage to keep up with him, Claire?'

'With difficulty sometimes,' she replied honestly. 'I always wish—' She broke off, realising in horror what she had been going to say, that she wished Ben had his father around to play with him. It was a relief when Ben came back with his football at that moment because it meant she could change the subject.

'Are you sure you want to bring that with you?' she asked, trying to inject a note of lightness into her voice.

'Course! Anyway, Sean's looking forward to playing another game, aren't you?' Ben demanded, turning to the man for confirmation.

'Oh, I can hardly wait!' Sean agreed, with such a rueful expression that they all laughed. However, there was a brooding quality to the look he gave Claire as he opened the car door for her, which made her suspect he might have realised what she had been going to say before Ben had interrupted…

She slid into the seat, closing her mind to that thought because she simply couldn't deal with it right then. Sean helped Ben into the booster seat in the back and made sure his seat belt was securely fastened, then slid behind the wheel. His expression held nothing more than friendliness when he looked at her.

'Right, then. Shall we be off? We have a bit of a drive ahead of us, although that's the *only* clue you're going to get about where we're going,' he teased.

Claire relaxed against the seat, letting all the tension seep from her body. It was obvious that Sean intended this to be nothing more than a pleasant day out for them all so she would sit back and enjoy it. 'I'm ready. How about you, Ben?'

'Yes!' Ben shouted gleefully.

Sean grinned as he started the engine. 'Then let's not waste any more time!'

It was a glorious day. Several hours later, stretched out in a comfy lounger, Claire found herself wondering when she'd last had so much fun.

Sean had driven them to the Lakes, parking at Lakeside so that they could catch the ferry to Bowness. Ben had been thrilled with such a treat but that had been only the start of it. Once they'd arrived at the town, Sean had led the way to the boatyard from where he had made arrangements to hire a motor-boat for the day.

Ben had been almost beside himself, strapping on the life-jacket he'd been given without a murmur. The boat was a beautiful little craft with a powerful engine and it had been obvious from the start that Sean knew how to handle it. They had done a full circuit of the lake then moored by the bank to have lunch. They had soon demolished the food she had brought and then Sean had agreed to play the much-vaunted game of football.

Claire had stayed behind on deck, content to watch their antics and even to doze a little in the surprisingly warm May sun. Frankly, she couldn't recall ever having spent such a pleasant and relaxing day...

She must have fallen fast asleep because the next thing she knew they were out in the centre of the lake again. She sat up, rubbing the sleep out of her eyes and blushing as she saw the grin Sean gave her.

'Woken up at last, have you, Sleeping Beauty? I was just beginning to wonder if I might have to use the tried and tested way of waking you from your slumbers,' he teased.

'Tried and tested...' she repeated, then blushed even harder as she realised what he'd meant.

'Uh-huh. It would have been no hardship either, Claire, waking you with a kiss.' He sighed ruefully. 'It's just a pity I'm not Prince Charming, I suppose.'

'Was...wasn't he in Cinderella?' she said hurriedly. A shiver ran through her and she gave a tinkly little laugh to disguise how it made her feel to imagine waking to the feel of Sean's mouth on hers. The worst thing of all was that she knew just how wonderful it would be because it had happened in the past. 'Wrong fairy-story, I'm afraid!'

'That's the story of my life, being in the wrong place at the wrong time. Or at least making the wrong *decision*.'

There was an edge to his voice all of a sudden which stirred up even more emotions. Claire knew he'd been alluding to his trip to Africa eight years before but she couldn't think what to say.

She looked round the deck instead, striving to keep her tone light. 'Where's Ben? You didn't throw him overboard for beating you at football again?'

'No. Although it did cross my mind!' Sean laughed as he slowed the boat to let one of the steamers pass.

'He's below, playing with that computer game he brought with him. I think he's tired, although he won't admit it.'

'I'm sure he is. It's been a lovely day, Sean. Thank you for going to so much trouble.'

'Thank you for coming with me. I've enjoyed it as well.' His hands tightened on the wheel, although he didn't look at her. 'I'd like to think that we could do it again, Claire—you, me and Ben. What do you think?'

It was on the tip of her tongue to agree until she realised how foolish it would be. She couldn't afford to let Sean get too close, although maybe it was already too late to stop that happening. Didn't she want to spend more time with him? Didn't her heart go cold at the thought of him leaving? Didn't that all add up to what she had avoided thinking about—that she still loved him?

The realisation washed over her in a cold wave of despair because she knew how pointless it was. No matter how much she loved Sean she could never tell him that! It just made the thought of his imminent departure all the harder to bear.

Misery kept her silent and she heard him sigh heavily. 'Sorry. I didn't mean to spoil things. You've made it clear that you aren't ready for another relationship even after all this time. Ben's father must have been quite a guy, Claire. Obviously, nobody else can ever match up to him in your eyes!'

Tears gathered in her eyes at the bitterness in his voice but she was powerless to do anything about it. When Sean announced that he thought it time they made their way back, she quietly agreed. Ben came up on deck just then, and it was a relief for both of them that the conversation had to be strictly confined to generalities.

Sean let the child pilot the boat, standing beside him and quietly explaining what he had to do as they headed back up the lake. Claire watched them with a lump in her throat. Sean was so patient, seemingly unfazed by Ben's unceasing questions. Ben would have learned so much from him if things had been different.

They took the ferry back to where Sean's car was parked. It had gone five by then and the car park was emptying fast. Sean stowed everything in the boot, leaving Claire to make sure that Ben was securely strapped in his seat. He turned on the radio as soon as they got back onto the A59, giving her the impression that he didn't want to talk.

She closed her eyes and pretended to sleep, glad that Ben had dropped off almost as soon as they had got under way. Much as she loved her son, she needed time to think, although her thoughts were so chaotic that it was impossible to unravel them…

'Hell's teeth! Did you hear that?'

The urgency in Sean's voice brought her eyes flying open, but when she started to ask him what was wrong he silenced her with shake of his head. Turning up the volume on the radio, he listened intently to the news bulletin that was being given out.

'Reports are coming in of a serious rail crash east of the town of Dalverston in northern Lancashire. Emergency services from both Lancashire and Cumbria have been drafted in to assist.

'Dalverston General Hospital, which is situated only a mile from the site of the crash, has issued a bulletin requesting that all staff report immediately for duty…'

'We'd better get back there as fast as we can.' Sean's tone was grim as he switched off the radio. He focused his attention solely on his driving from then on so that it seemed no time at all before they were turning into her road.

He drew up in front of her house and turned to her. 'Will you be coming in to work?'

'Of course, as long as I can get Mrs Mitchell to look after Ben.' She glanced at the child who had just woken up. 'OK, love, let's get going.'

They both got out of the car but Ben hung behind. 'Are you going to the crash, Sean?' he asked worriedly.

'Yes. There are a lot of people hurt and they need all the help they can get, Ben,' he explained quietly.

'But you'll be careful, won't you?' the boy insisted. He glanced at Claire. 'And you'll make sure Mum is careful, too?'

Sean's voice was very deep as he looked at her. 'I'll take good care of your mother, Ben. Trust me.'

The child seemed reassured by that and ran up the path. Claire struggled to find enough breath to speak but her head was reeling. Sean had made it sound almost as though he were making a vow…

'I'll see you down there,' she said hurriedly, turning away because the desire to linger was too strong. She heard the car drive off as she let herself into the house, but she concentrated on what she had to do rather than anything else. If Sean had meant that as something more than it might have at first seemed then this certainly wasn't the time to go into it!

'Right, I want you, Sean, to go in the next ambulance with Claire. We've enough staff here now to allow us to send more out to the crash site itself.'

Dr Hill, who was directing operations, turned to her. 'You know the ropes, Claire. We work this as we've rehearsed in case we had a major incident in our area.

There are half a dozen ambulance crews down there, ferrying the injured, but they need someone to act as triage nurse. We must make sure that the most seriously injured are attended to with as little delay as possible.'

'I understand.' Claire didn't waste time on questions as she hurriedly made her way to the supply room where all the equipment was kept. Sean followed her inside, whistling as he saw the array stored in there.

'I'm impressed,' he admitted, taking the waterproof jacket and trousers she gave him. He pulled them on over his clothes then selected a hard hat from the shelf. 'How come you're this well prepared?'

'It was decided about six months ago that we had to upgrade our equipment in case of an emergency like this,' she explained, pulling on her own protective clothing. 'We're only a few miles from the motorway and it's one of the busiest interchanges so it was thought that any problems would come from there.'

'But instead it's turned out to be the railway? You can never tell, can you?' he observed, following her outside to the waiting ambulance. He nodded to Joe Henderson and Jenny Partridge, who were manning it. 'OK, ready when you are. How is it out there?'

'Grim,' Jenny told him succinctly.

They set off with sirens blaring so that it took them very little time to reach the site of the crash. Claire stepped down from the ambulance, barely able to absorb what she was seeing.

The train's engine had left the track, dragging several of the carriages down a steep embankment with it. Two carriages were piled one on top of the other and she could see firemen preparing to use lifting gear to separate them, after the injured had been dealt with. It was growing dark and arc lights had been set up around the site. The light they gave out added a surreal quality to the scene of devastation.

'The most badly injured are down there, in the lower of those two carriages,' Joe Henderson explained. 'It's a bloody nightmare, I'm afraid. There must be several dozen people still trapped in there.'

'Then we'd better get down there and see what we can do. Claire?' Sean held out his hand, gripping hers firmly as they began to descend the slippery embankment. Claire held her breath, afraid that one false step would send her tumbling into the tangle of metal below. However, Sean never wavered as he led her safely down to the bottom.

He let her go, taking swift stock of the situation as he looked round. 'I'll go and have a word with the fire chief and see what the situation is regarding those still trapped inside the carriages.'

'Right.' Claire glanced at the group of injured sitting or lying on the ground beside the track. 'I'll go and check this lot over and see who needs urgent treatment.'

'Fine. Be careful, though, won't you? Don't go taking any risks.'

She gave him a quick smile, not deaf to the concern in his voice. 'And you be careful, too, Sean.'

'I shall.' He touched her cheek with his gloved hand then headed over to where the fire officers were discussing what to do next. Claire took a quick breath but it did nothing to slow the rapid beating of her heart as she recalled the gentleness of his touch and the expression in his eyes. She hurried over to the casualties, deliberately blanking her mind to all else but what needed to be done. There would be time to think about everything else later.

By the time Sean came back she had worked her way

through the group and was confident that there was no one who needed urgent treatment. Most had suffered cuts and grazes plus the odd fracture, which she had dealt with temporarily. All were deeply shocked, but their injuries weren't life-threatening.

Sean nodded as she finished her report. 'Fine. The ambulances can ferry them to hospital as soon as they get back. The less badly injured are being taken to the Royal to leave Dalverston free to deal with the more serious cases.'

He looked round as someone hailed him and went to meet the policeman who was hurrying towards them. Claire followed, knowing that there was little more she could do for this group. She could hear sirens approaching and knew they would be on their way to hospital within a very short time.

'He's under a seat. He doesn't look too badly injured but the fire crew want someone to check him over before they move him. Can you come, Doc?' the policeman was saying to Sean when she reached them.

'Sure,' Sean agreed, then turned to her. 'There's a child trapped in the lower carriage. Can you come with me, Claire? I might need a hand.'

'Of course.' She didn't ask any questions as she hurried after him. The police officer led the way, pointing to a ladder which had been put against the side of the carriage.

'The only way in is through a broken skylight as most of the doors are jammed. You'll have to take it carefully, though, as there's a lot of glass and jagged metal about,' he warned them.

'Right.' Sean set off up the ladder, waiting at the top as Claire climbed up after him. The noise was tremendous as the emergency services used high-powered oxyacetylene torches to cut through the metal, making normal speech impossible.

Sean cupped his hand to her ear. 'I'll go in first and see what we need. You wait here.'

She nodded to let him know that she understood, watching tensely as he slid through the skylight. A light had been rigged up inside and she saw him crouch down beside one of the seats. He looked up, raising his voice so that it would carry above the din.

'He doesn't look too bad, Claire. I'll need a neck brace and some saline. He's got a nasty cut on his arm which is bleeding rather heavily. OK?'

She gave him a thumbs-up to show she understood, then carefully climbed down the ladder and told the policeman what they needed. He took her over to where a small pile of medical supplies had been stacked, waiting while she found what she needed. He followed her up the ladder, passing her the neck brace, which she dropped into Sean's outstretched hands.

It was awkward, trying to fit it in such a confined space, but, with the help of one of the firemen, Sean managed it at last. The child was crying listlessly and he spoke soothingly to it all the while but it had little effect. He looked up at Claire, his face eerily pale in the glow from the spotlights.

'I'm going to pass him up to you. There's no way I can get the drip into him down here. Are you ready?'

She nodded and leaned into the opening as Sean lifted the child up towards her. It was a little boy, about four years old, and as soon as she saw him Claire's heart turned over because it was obvious that he had Down's syndrome.

She passed him to the police officer then quickly followed him down the ladder. 'Put him down here on the grass, can you? I need to set up a drip.'

She worked quickly as she set up the IV line, all the time wondering if the child knew what was happening. There were different degrees of Down's syndrome and it was impossible to tell how badly affected he was.

He cried steadily throughout, tears dripping down his pale checks, and she looked at the policeman in concern.

'What's happened to his mother? Do you know?'

'I've no idea. She might have been taken to hospital. There were several women amongst the last lot they got out—she could have been one of them.' He cast a pitying glance at the little boy. 'Poor kid, I expect he's wondering what's going on and where his mum is.'

'Mummy…' Whether the boy recognised the word or it was just coincidence, he suddenly began calling for her. Claire stroked the damp hair back from his forehead, murmuring soothingly.

'Shh, poppet, it's all right. Mummy won't be long.' She looked round as Sean suddenly appeared and lowered her voice. 'Where do you think his mother is? She wouldn't have left him alone so what do you think has happened to her? Do you think she might have been taken to hospital already?'

'I'll check to see if they got her out earlier. The child was wedged right under the seat so no one realised he was there until they heard him crying. If the mother was unconscious, she wouldn't have been able to tell them, would she?' he said tersely, getting up to hurry over to the officer in charge of operations.

He shook his head as he came back. 'No. He's certain that she wasn't taken out of this section of carriage. Evidently there was a couple of elderly folk, a man and his wife, but that's all…'

He broke off as a sudden shout from inside the carriage set off a flurry of activity. Several firemen raced to the ladder and ran up it. The fire chief came hurrying over to them. 'We've found a young woman trapped in the toilets. She's in a pretty bad way, too. Can you come?'

They both got to their feet, although Claire hesitated as she glanced at the little boy. However, just at that moment Jenny came slithering down the embankment. 'I believe you've got a child for us…' She broke off with a gasp of horror. 'It's Robbie!'

'You know who he is?' Claire demanded.

'Yes, of course. He's Laura's little boy…Laura Grady. She used to work on the maternity unit.' Jenny looked round in concern. 'Where is she? She would never leave Robbie on his own like this if she could help it.'

'We think she may be still inside the carriage,' Sean explained grimly. 'There's a young woman trapped in the toilet and evidently she's in a pretty bad way.'

'Oh, I do hope it isn't Laura!' Jenny exclaimed, looking upset. 'If anything happens to her, who'll look after Robbie? His father died a few months ago, you see, and there's only Laura…' She tailed off but she didn't need to say anything else as the situation was perfectly clear to all of them.

Sean's face was set into lines of determination as he turned to Claire. 'Let's go.'

Leaving Jenny to take little Robbie to the hospital, Claire quickly followed him. It was awkward, dropping down into the carriage, but Sean helped her as much as he could. They were met by a couple of firemen who looked very grave.

'She's through here. We haven't been able to get to

her yet as the lavatory door is jammed halfway open. But it doesn't look good, from what we can see. Just mind where you're stepping. There's a lot of jagged metal about in here.'

It was difficult, easing through the twisted metal, but they made it at last and then Claire could see why it was proving such a problem to get to the injured woman. Not only was the lavatory door jammed by some unseen obstruction, but part of the carriage wall had been stoved in with the force of the crash and was blocking the area directly in front of it. Two firemen were cutting through the metal but it was a slow process and so far they had only succeeded in making a very narrow gap.

Sean dropped to his knees and peered through the gap. 'I can see her. I'll just see if I can reach her…' He stretched his arm as far as it would go into the space then shook his head. 'Damn! I can't get any further. But she looks in a bad way all right. How long will it be before your men can cut away this section?'

'About fifteen minutes. But then we still have to remove whatever is jamming the toilet door. I'd guess that the basin has come away from the wall and that's what's causing it so we may need to cut the door away as well,' the fireman explained.

'We really need to move on this. I don't like the look of her at all,' Sean said in concern.

'Maybe I can squeeze through that gap,' Claire suggested. 'I'm smaller than you so I might just fit if I took off this jacket.'

'No, it's too risky,' he said at once. 'That section is very unstable and you could be crushed.'

'We can't leave her there and do nothing, Sean!' she declared, unzipping the heavy yellow reflective jacket. 'I'm going to give it a shot anyhow.'

She could tell that he wasn't happy but he knew as well as she did that every second wasted increased the risk to the young woman. Once she had shed the jacket and the equally bulky trousers, Claire lay down flat and began inching her way through the gap. It was a tight squeeze but she made it, hunching herself up as she tucked herself into a tiny space alongside the injured woman.

She quickly took the woman's pulse, forcing herself to concentrate on what she was doing although the noise of the oxyacetylene cutters was deafening.

'Pulse is very faint and rapid,' she shouted to Sean. 'But she's breathing OK.'

'Right. Check for any external signs of injury,' he instructed tersely.

Claire ran her hands over the woman's skull, feeling for any signs of depression or swelling, but there weren't any. Next she checked the arms and legs. There was heavy bruising on her left thigh and the area was grossly distended. Claire grimaced when she saw it.

'Definite fracture of the left thigh bone and she's losing a lot of blood, from the look of it.'

She broke off as the woman's eyes fluttered open. 'What happened? Where am I…?' She suddenly gasped. 'Robbie!'

Claire pressed her down as she tried to sit up. 'Keep still. Robbie is fine. He's been taken to Dalverston General but he isn't badly hurt. He's just got a cut on his arm,' she explained, deliberately making light of the child's injuries. 'We have to concentrate on getting you out of here now.'

'Will it take long? I want to be with Robbie. He isn't used to me not being there.' Once again the woman tried to sit up and cried out in pain.

'You've got a fractured thigh bone and maybe a slight concussion.' Claire pressed her gently back down again. 'You have to lie still otherwise you're going to make things worse for yourself.'

'I just can't bear to think of Robbie being on his own in a strange place.' Tears trickled down the woman's pretty face. Claire patted her hand, understanding only too well how anxious she was to be with her child. She would have felt the same if Ben had been injured.

'I know you do but you must be sensible. It's Laura, isn't it? Jenny Partridge recognised Robbie and told me your name. She said that you used to be a nurse so you know better than anyone how important it is that you do as we tell you.'

She smiled as Laura nodded. 'Right, I'm going to get a line into you to replace some of that fluid and then we'll take it from there. OK?'

'OK, but tell them to hurry… Robbie needs me…'

Laura's eyes closed as she suddenly lapsed back into unconsciousness. Claire quickly checked her pulse and went weak with relief when she found it, although it was fainter than it had been a few minutes earlier. It was obvious that Laura was suffering from shock and blood loss and she knew that they needed to get her to hospital as quickly as possible. In the meantime, they simply had to do all they could to keep her stable.

The next hour seemed to drag. Claire rigged up an IV line to replace some of the lost fluid then set about protecting the injured limb from further damage by wrapping it in padding which Sean passed through the gap to her. He also managed to get a thermal blanket to her as well, and she covered Laura with it, praying that it would help maintain her body heat.

Laura drifted in and out of consciousness and each

time it seemed that her level of responsiveness was lower. It was extremely worrying for everyone concerned. Claire knew that she had never felt so helpless in the whole of her life.

The firemen finally managed to cut away the buckled section of carriage and then they set to work on the lavatory door as it was impossible to free it any other way.

Claire was given a mask to protect her eyes from the glare of the oxyacetylene torch and a cover to protect her and Laura from the heat of the flame, but she was thankful when it was finally over.

It took Sean plus three of the firemen to manhandle the stretcher through the wrecked compartment. They had strapped Laura securely to it and passed her up through the skylight, where a dozen helping hands were waiting to receive her. However, it was Sean who helped Claire out and down the ladder, his hands that steadied her as she stumbled with fatigue on reaching the bottom.

'Are you all right, darling?' he asked solicitously, earning himself a shaky smile which owed its tremor as much to the endearment as anything else.

'Just about...' She gave a little shudder of reaction and heard him utter something under his breath as he reached out and enfolded her in his arms.

'Good job, you two. Well done!'

Lee Aspinall, who had struggled from his sickbed to help out, shouted as he passed them. Sean gave him a wave then slowly, and with the utmost reluctance, let her go.

'Let's see how Laura is and then we'll check if we're still needed here.' He looked round and sighed. 'It looks as though everyone is accounted for now, thank heavens.'

Claire silently agreed as she accompanied him to the waiting ambulance, where Laura was lying on a stretcher. Claire climbed in beside her and took her hand as the other woman's eyes opened.

'Hi, there. How are you doing?' she asked softly.

'Fine...thanks to you.' Laura's voice was thready with fatigue and the effects of the painkiller she had been given. 'Want to thank you... Anything happened to me then who would look after Robbie...?'

Her eyes closed once again. Claire climbed out of the ambulance, standing stiffly as Sean closed the doors. All of a sudden the parallel between Laura's situation and her own seemed to hit her.

Who would look after Ben if anything happened to her? she wondered sickly. Her parents were dead now and she had no other family apart from a few distant cousins she had lost touch with. If she wasn't around then Ben would be all on his own.

'Right, that's it. Everyone is accounted for and all the injured have been taken to hospital.' Sean came back at that moment and she struggled to rid herself of the deeply disquieting thought, but it was impossible to erase it.

If Sean noticed her distraction he obviously put it down to tiredness as they made their way to the police car which was to ferry them back to the hospital. She sat in the back, barely listening as Sean and the police officer discussed what had gone on that night. She kept thinking about what would happen to Ben if she weren't there to look after him. The thought that he would have nobody to turn to, nobody to love and cherish him, was almost too much.

'Claire?'

She jumped as Sean said her name, realising with a

start that they were parked in the hospital forecourt. She let him help her out of the car, adding her thanks for the lift in a flat little voice which brought a frown to Sean's face.

'Are you all right?' he asked softly as the car zoomed away.

'Of course,' she quickly assured him, but she could tell he didn't believe her.

It didn't take long to report back and hand in their equipment, then they were free to leave. It was almost one a.m., she was shocked to discover as they walked out to the car park together. Sean stopped beside his car, unlocked the passenger door and turned to her.

'I'll run you home.'

'But I've got my own car—' she began, but he interrupted her curtly.

'Leave it here, Claire. You're in no fit state to drive.' His face held an expression which warned her he wasn't going to take no for an answer, and suddenly she was too tired to argue.

She slid into the seat and closed her eyes, letting her head drop back as Sean started the engine. It seemed to take no time at all before he was drawing up outside her house. Ben was staying with Mrs Mitchell for the night because Claire hadn't been sure what time she would get back, and suddenly the thought of going into the empty house was more than she could bear.

She turned to Sean before she had time to reconsider. 'Would you like to come in? I could make us some coffee or something…' She tailed off because she simply couldn't continue as she saw the expression in his eyes. Suddenly, her heart was racing, the blood rushing through her veins as he continued to look at her steadily.

'If I come in, Claire, it won't be for coffee. I think we both know that.'

His voice sounded unusually harsh but she knew that was because he was trying his best to disguise how important this was to him. A wave of tenderness ran through her and she smiled at him, unaware that her heart was in her eyes at that moment.

'Maybe we can give coffee a miss this time, Sean?' she said softly.

CHAPTER TEN

THEY made it into the hall but that was as far as they got. Their hunger for each other was just too great to be denied even a second longer.

Sean pressed her back against the door as he rained kisses over her face and neck. Claire murmured in pleasure, delighting in the feel of his lips on her skin, the pressure of his strong body against hers. It was a homecoming in every sense of the word.

'Claire!' He said her name with such passion and yet such tenderness that her heart melted. She slid her arms around his neck and looked deep into his eyes, smiling as she saw the flames that lit them.

'Sean?' she teased, marvelling that she could manage to do that when her body was burning up with desire. Yet there was something deeply sensual about putting off the inevitable that little bit longer.

'Think it's funny to tease a guy *in extremis*, do you?' he growled, swinging her up into his arms so fast that she gasped. He took her mouth in a deliberately provocative kiss then smiled into her eyes. 'I think you need a taste of your own medicine, Sister Shepherd.'

'Oh, is that a fact?' She gave the smallest shrug, hearing his swiftly indrawn breath as her breast brushed his arm. Her smile was just the tiniest bit smug as she looked into his passion-darkened eyes. 'Is that a threat or a promise, Dr Fitzgerald?'

'Either … both … whatever … you … want … it … to …

be!' He punctuated each word with a kiss then grinned complacently as he saw the effect he'd had. 'Make up your mind.'

She would have been hard-pressed to string two sensible thoughts together at that moment, and she knew that he was aware of it! Claire contented herself with what was meant to be a haughty glare, but the way he laughed told her how miserably she'd failed.

He brushed his lips against hers, drawing back before she had time to respond, and this time there was very little amusement in his voice. 'As I said, this can be whatever you want it to be, my love. I'm not going to press you into doing something you'll come to regret.'

He took a deep breath and it sounded as though the words had been forced from him. 'I can stay here tonight just as a friend, if that's what you want.'

Her eyes misted with tears at his thoughtfulness. She shook her head, 'That isn't what I want, Sean. I want you here as a friend, of course, but I also want you as…as a lover.'

Her voice broke on the last word but he was already bending to take her mouth in a kiss of such passion and need that there was no time to worry about it. He wanted her and she wanted him—it was all that mattered at that moment.

He carried her upstairs and laid her down on her bed with a tenderness that brought a lump to her throat. That this was as important to Sean as it was to her was beyond question. The evidence was clear to see in the way he looked at her, in how his hands trembled as he began to unfasten her blouse. He was usually deft but now his hands shook so much that the tiny pearl buttons defeated him.

'Let me,' Claire offered, gently pushing his hands

aside while she undid the buttons. She stopped after she'd undone the last one, suddenly shy about going any further. It had been such a long time since Sean had seen her naked, and she'd had Ben since then. What if he didn't find her attractive any longer? What if he was disappointed by the changes in her body?

'You're beautiful, Claire.' His voice was tender as he parted the front of her blouse and let his eyes rest on her breasts, barely hidden by the lacy bra she wore. 'You were beautiful all those years ago and you're even more beautiful now.'

How had he known what she'd been thinking? she wondered as he bent and kissed the soft swell of her breasts.

The answer came to her immediately, flowing out of the darkness, filling her with warmth and comfort. Sean loved her and that was why he had no difficulty in understanding her fears. It was probably the most poignant moment of all to realise it. Suddenly, any uncertainties she'd had disappeared. This was the turning point and from here on things would work out!

She gave the softest murmur, seeing the concern in his eyes as he saw the tears that misted her eyes. 'Claire, darling, what is it—?' he began, but she silenced him with a kiss that left no room for any more questions. There would be time enough for them later.

They hadn't drawn the curtains and the silvery moonlight flowing through the window added an extra magic to their love-making. The sight of Sean's strong, naked body bathed in its soft light made her pulse race and her blood flow hotly through her veins as she watched him shed his clothes. He came back to lie beside her, his hands once more deft as he quickly stripped away her clothing. They only trembled slightly as he slid the silky panties down her hips but, then, she was trembling, too.

He stared at her with the eyes of one to whom the sight was almost too beautiful to bear. Slowly, so slowly, he let his fingertips trail down her from throat to thigh, releasing a frisson of heat inside her which made her shudder. His hand came to rest on the soft inner flesh of her thigh as his eyes held hers in a look which seemed to encompass everything both of them were feeling.

'I love you, Claire. I've always loved you. I…I just wanted you to know that…first.'

He slid down beside her, his hands tender yet urgent as they stroked her body, setting up a chain of reactions which soon had her twisting helplessly against the cool cotton cover.

'Sean…please,' she murmured, reaching up to draw him towards her. Her breath exhaled on a sigh of pleasure as she felt his weight settle over her, but it was only a taste of the pleasure to come. She had wondered once if making love with Sean would be a familiar experience or something new, but it was both. Her body recognised his at once and yet there was a newness and urgency about their love-making which added an extra dimension. Nothing could have prepared her for the sheer depth of joy she felt when they joined in the ultimate act of giving between two people…

Claire awoke slowly, her body languorous after the night she had spent in Sean's arms. It had been almost dawn before they had drifted off to sleep, too tired to make love any more. She had slept heavily after that, content in the knowledge that he was beside her, his arm heavy and comforting as it lay across her.

Now she reached out to touch him, wanting the pleasure of feeling his warmth beside her, but the bed was empty and the sheets were cold. She shivered as she sat up and looked around, seeing immediately that his clothes were gone. Surely he hadn't left?

It seemed inconceivable after the night they had spent together and the closeness it had brought. She had made up her mind at some point during the hours they had lain in each other's arms that she would tell him the truth this morning about Ben. Sean would understand because they were now so in tune that he would realise *why* she had felt it necessary to do what she had. Yet as she looked around the empty room she felt the first stirring of uncertainty.

She tossed back the bedclothes, determined not to let it get out of hand. She had to tell Sean the truth after last night, and it was as simple as that. She hurried into the bathroom to shower then dressed quickly in jeans and a sweater, before running downstairs.

There was no sign of him in the kitchen but the smell of fresh coffee proved that he must be somewhere about. He would hardly have stopped to make coffee if he'd been intent on hurrying off! she reasoned. The uncertainty she had felt receded then disappeared altogether as the back door opened and both Ben and Sean appeared.

'Hi, you two. What have you been up to?' she said, smiling at them. Then felt her heart skip a beat as she saw the expression on Sean's face. What was the matter with him? she wondered sickly as all her fears came flooding back. Why was he looking at her like that with such…such contempt?

'I took Sean down to see the donkeys 'cos he hadn't seen them before,' Ben explained, referring to the nearby donkey sanctuary, which was one of his favourite places to visit. 'I took them some bread, Mum. Was that all right?'

'Of course.' She managed to smile but Sean's continued silence was making her nervous. 'You should have woken me up and I could have come with you.'

'Oh, Sean said that you were tired and that we should let you have a lie-in,' Ben assured her. 'I 'spect it was having to help all those people last night, wasn't it, Mum?'

A touch of colour bloomed in her cheeks and she looked away, uncomfortable with the innocent question. 'Probably. Anyway, you'd better go upstairs and wash your hands ready for church.'

'Do I have to go?' Ben wheedled. 'I'd rather stay here with Sean.'

'I'll be leaving soon. There are a few things I need to do.' Sean smiled at the child but she was conscious of the edge in his voice even if Ben appeared blissfully unaware of it.

'Oh. Well, I suppose I'll have to go, then. But I'll see you soon, won't I, Sean?' Ben demanded.

'If you don't hurry up you'll be late,' Claire cut in quickly, painfully conscious that Sean hadn't answered the question. She waited until Ben had gone reluctantly upstairs before she turned to him. 'What is it, Sean? What's wrong?'

'I don't know what you mean,' he denied, looking around him. 'Do you know where I left my car keys? I can't seem to find them.'

'They could be in the hall.' She caught his arm as he went to walk past her, unable to disguise her hurt and fear at the way he was acting. 'Please, tell me what's happened, Sean. Last night I thought…well, I thought it meant something!'

'So did I!' His eyes blazed, full of a bitter anger which made her go cold when she saw it. 'But then I thought that what we shared all those years ago meant something, too. Just goes to show how wrong you can be, doesn't it?'

'I don't understand what you're saying, Sean! You're not making sense…' She stopped as he caught hold of her. His fingers bit into the soft flesh of her upper arms yet she knew that he wasn't aware that he was hurting her.

'That's where you're wrong! For the first time in eight years everything suddenly makes sense.' He gave a bitter laugh which made her feel sick. 'No wonder you refused to go with me, sweetheart. I always wondered why you changed your mind at the last moment but it just goes to show what a fool I was for not reading the signs.'

Her heart was hammering so hard that it was difficult to think straight. Yet one thought reared itself up through the confusion—had Sean found out about Ben? Was that what this was all about? It was the only explanation she could come up with.

'You know about Ben, don't you?' she said softly, watching his face so that she saw the pain which flickered across it.

He abruptly let her go, turning so that she couldn't see his expression any longer. 'Yes, I know, Claire. What's that saying about out of the mouths of babes?' He gave a harsh laugh but she could see the shudder that ran through him and it confused her. Sean was angry, as he had a right to be, but why did he appear so…so distraught?

Her heart skipped a beat as she considered the answer. Didn't Sean want Ben to be his son? Was that it? But before she could decide what to say he carried on in a tone that was devoid of emotion.

'Ben told me that it's his birthday next month and that he'll be eight. He had no idea, of course, what that would mean to me.' He suddenly swung round and his gaze was so bitter that she took an instinctive step back.

'It didn't take much working out to realize that Ben must have been conceived during the time we were together, Claire. What I can't understand is why you didn't tell me that you had met someone else. Did you think I'd create a scene? Or were you trying to be kind by letting me go overseas, ignorant of the fact that you were having some other man's child?'

'I…I…' Words were beyond her as he stood there, accusing her of the worst kind of infidelity possible. Did he really believe that she could have done that to him, had a relationship with another man while she'd been seeing him?

It beggared belief, stole her ability to respond to the accusation he had hurled at her, and he obviously took her silence as proof that he was right.

He walked to the kitchen door then paused to look back, and she felt her heart ache with a pain so intense that it felt as though it were breaking as she saw the bleakness in his eyes. 'I wish you'd told me the truth, Claire. Maybe you did it to spare my feelings but I would have preferred to know. It doesn't sit well, knowing what a fool I've been these past few weeks hoping that we could pick up where we left off.'

He gave the softest laugh. 'There's nothing to pick up, is there, Claire? I've been fantasising about something that never even existed.'

'No! You're wrong, Sean.' She took a deep breath. Her thoughts were in such a jumble that she couldn't think how to convince him. 'What about last night? That wasn't a fantasy!'

'Wasn't it?' He took a deep breath. 'Last night I made love to a woman who doesn't exist, Claire. If that isn't a fantasy then I don't know what is.'

He turned and walked away, and a few moments later she heard the front door closing. She stayed right where she was, unable to move. Maybe later she would think of all the things she should have said to him, starting with the truth about Ben. But right at that moment she couldn't think of anything.

'I'm surprised that Sean has handed in his notice. I thought he would apply for Juliet Carmichael's job now that it's been advertised. Although I suppose he is rather over-qualified for it, wouldn't you say, Claire?'

'I...I suppose so.' Claire summoned a smile, aware that Margaret was watching her closely. Was the rift between her and Sean so apparent that everyone had noticed? she wondered.

In the two weeks since Sean had walked out of her house, they had spoken barely half a dozen words to one another, and those had been out of necessity. Sean had been asked to change shifts to cover for Lee Aspinall, who had developed pneumonia as a result of leaving his sickbed to attend the train crash. It meant that they had seen each other only briefly in passing, but even those meetings had been painful.

Sean had treated her with such indifference that it had felt as though someone had been systematically ripping another bit off her heart each time. Claire had done her best not to let him see how hurtful she found it, but it hadn't been easy. Maybe it was for the best if Sean left sooner than expected?

'You OK, Claire? You're looking all...well...all broody again.' Margaret lowered her voice so that nobody could overhear. 'Have you and Sean had some sort of falling out?'

It was pointless to deny it so she shrugged. 'You could say that. Still, I hope he'll be very happy wherever he goes. He's a good doctor.'

'Uh-huh.'

For once Margaret didn't press the point and Claire was grateful. She gave the older woman a quick smile. 'Right, I'm going to pop in to see how Robbie and Laura are doing, instead of taking my break. You know where I am if you need me.'

'Okey-dokey.' Margaret bustled off to see to an elderly man who had tripped over a paving stone as Claire hurried away. She took the lift to the third floor because her time was limited but she had promised Laura that she would call in and see her as soon as she got a chance. They had struck up a friendship in the past two weeks and Claire looked forward to their chats. It helped put her own troubles into perspective when she thought about the problems Laura had to deal with.

She stopped off at the children's ward on the way to see Robbie and discovered that he already had a visitor. The pretty blonde woman, carrying a plump blonde baby girl, smiled as Claire appeared.

'Ah, I think this must be Aunty Claire, isn't it, Robbie?'

'Yes!' Robbie hurled himself across the bed to hug Claire, almost strangling her in his delight at seeing her again. Claire laughed as she hugged his sturdy little body to her. Robbie loved everyone—the nurses, the doctors, the cleaners—everyone! He treated them all to the same unbridled show of affection. He should have been discharged by now but she knew that a few rules had been bent so that he could remain in the hospital until Laura was well enough to be discharged.

Now she popped him on her knee and produced the packet of fruit chews she'd brought with her, and he was soon happily munching away.

'I think these are his favourites,' she told the other woman with a laugh. 'Although he loves chocolate buttons as well.'

'Robbie loves most sweets, don't you, poppet?' The woman ruffled his hair then smiled at Claire. 'I'm Sarah Gillespie, by the way. And this is my daughter, Becky.'

'It's nice to meet you both. I take it that you're friends of Laura's?' Claire asked, putting Robbie down so that he could go and hug the ward cleaner who had just arrived.

'Mmm. I used to work on the maternity unit before this little madam appeared. My husband is Niall Gillespie, the Chief of Obstetrics,' she added in a voice which said everything that needed to be said about that.

Claire felt a pang of envy at the blatant happiness in Sarah's voice as she'd mentioned her husband. 'I see. Did you meet him when you worked there?'

'Yes. Niall took over the post after the previous chap retired.' Sarah laughed softly. 'We had rather a rocky start to our relationship. Let's just say that Niall didn't seem to approve of me,' she explained as Claire's brows rose. 'However, I managed to change his mind, I'm glad to say! We've been married well over a year now and it's been the most wonderful time of my life, especially since Becky arrived. Are you married, Claire? Do you have children?'

'I'm not married but I do have a son, Ben. He's almost eight,' she added.

Sarah sighed. 'It must be difficult, being on your own

and bringing up a child. I know I'd find it hard. And as for Laura…well, I don't know how she copes. Ian, her husband, died last year and it's been a struggle for her, financially and emotionally. She was just trying to get her life back together when the accident happened.'

'The only thing she was worried about was Robbie. She didn't seem at all concerned about herself but who would look after him if anything happened to her.' Claire bit her lip because it was painful to think back and recall how she had felt at that time. It was hard to believe that she had been on the verge of telling Sean the truth…

'Hey! Are you OK?' Sarah frowned in concern as she saw the glimmer of tears in her eyes.

'Yes, of course…' she began, then shook her head. 'No, not really. I'm sorry.'

'Don't apologise. Look, let's tell Robbie we're leaving and go and have a cup of coffee in the canteen.' Sarah shook her head when Claire started to object. 'No. It's obvious that you need someone to talk to and I'm more than willing to listen. Most problems are never that bad once you talk about them.'

'Well…' Maybe she should have politely refused, but all of a sudden Claire knew that she needed to talk to someone about what had happened, and who better than this woman who was virtually a stranger to her? They both said goodbye to Robbie and left him happily dusting the bedside lockers with one of the cleaner's yellow dusters.

The canteen was almost empty so they chose a table by the window. Sarah smiled as she handed Claire her baby. 'Here, you hold Becky for me, will you? I'll fetch the coffee.'

Claire cuddled the child to her as Sarah hurried to the

counter, taking comfort from the feel of the plump little body in her arms.

'Right, come on, get it all off your chest. You'll feel better, I promise you,' Sarah instructed, putting two brimming cups on the table in front of them as she sat down. Claire took a deep breath but suddenly it was surprisingly easy to talk about everything she had kept secret for so long. Maybe the desire to talk about it had been building up over the years so that it was a relief to get it all out into the open at last.

Sarah cleared her throat when Claire had finished, obviously moved by the tale. 'You must have loved Sean an awful lot to have done what you did, Claire. It took guts to go it alone so that he wouldn't have to give up his dreams.'

'I do,' she said simply.

Sarah smiled. '"Do", not "did"? So you still love him, then?'

Claire looked down at the sleeping baby in her arms. 'Yes. I...I've always loved him.' She looked up and the truth was plain to see in her eyes. 'I've never loved anyone but Sean and I never shall.'

'And he told you that he loved you?' When she nodded Sarah smiled. 'Then it seems to me that the pair of you need your heads banged together! What more do you need? For heaven's sake, Claire, tell him how you feel, tell him that he was wrong about Ben. Tell him the *truth* because it's way past time you did that, from the sound of it. If Sean Fitzgerald is half the man I think he is then he'll want to hear it!'

'I don't know... I'm not sure if it's a good idea,' Claire hedged, her heart stumbling at the thought. 'What if he doesn't want to listen? What if he won't believe me? What if—?'

'What if you tell him the one thing he wants to hear more than anything else? Be positive. *Think* positive!' Sarah reached across the table and squeezed her hand. 'I know how scared you are because I've been there. It wasn't plain sailing for Niall and me either, but sometimes all it needs is that little bit of extra courage to admit how you feel and then the rest is easy. Problems have a funny way of working themselves out.'

She finished her coffee then stood up and smiled at Claire as she took the baby from her. 'I'm not going to say anything else. It's up to you now, Claire. But I expect an invitation to the wedding if things work out the way I think they will!'

Sarah left the canteen and after a few minutes Claire followed her. It was now too late to go and see Laura so she went back to the department. There was the usual influx of patients all afternoon long so she was kept busy, dealing with them. But she couldn't stop thinking about what Sarah Gillespie had said, and *how* she had said it with such conviction.

Was there a way to work this out if she had the courage to try? By the time she went off duty she still hadn't decided.

Ben was very quiet over tea. He bolted his food down then went rushing up to his room and stayed there most of the evening. Claire was so distracted that she barely registered his strange behaviour. Her mind kept twisting and turning as she tried to decide if she should take Sarah's advice.

She was so worn out with thinking about it that she went to bed just after ten then lay awake, worrying some more. She must have dropped off to sleep at last, only to be woken a short time later by a crash from the next room.

She leapt out of bed and hurried into Ben's room to find him lying on the floor, struggling for breath. He was wheezing heavily and his lips were already faintly blue.

'It's all right, darling. I'll get your inhaler,' she told him, running to the chest of drawers to fetch it. She went and knelt beside him, propping him up against her. 'Now, try to exhale first then take a slow, deep breath.'

Ben tried to do as she'd said but his airway was in such spasm that it was impossible for him to take in the full quantity of bronchodilating drug.

Claire clamped down on her own panic, knowing that it would only make things worse. 'We'll have another try, sweetheart. Just try to relax. Ready?'

Once again they tried to get enough of the drug into his airway to relax the constricted muscles, but it was obvious from the child's blue-tinged lips and heaving chest that it hadn't worked. Claire piled a mound of pillows behind him and got up, realising that she couldn't delay any longer.

'I'm going to phone for an ambulance, Ben. Just try to relax—don't fight it. We'll soon have you sorted out.' She ran downstairs and dialled 999, trying to contain her panic as she gave her address to the operator. She couldn't recall him ever having an attack as severe as this one and couldn't imagine what had triggered it.

Ben seemed no worse when she went back to him but he didn't seem any better either. His face was pale and clammy with perspiration, his heartbeat far too rapid, and he was wheezing heavily. It was a huge relief when the ambulance arrived and he was immediately given oxygen, which helped a little.

The drive to the hospital seemed to take for ever, although Claire knew that it was only a few minutes. She'd had time only to drag a coat over her pyjamas and slip her feet into some shoes before she'd left, but how she looked was the least of her worries. She held Ben's hand as the paramedics rushed the trolley in through the doors.

'Claire! What's happened?'

She spun round at the sound of Sean's voice, the tears she'd held in check starting to pour down her face. 'It's Ben. He's had an asthma attack…' She couldn't continue as a sob broke from her lips.

'He'll be all right, my love.' Sean gripped her hand for a moment as the crew pushed Ben into the trauma unit. 'I promise you that I won't let anything happen to him.'

'I know you won't.' She pressed a trembling hand to her mouth as Sean hurried away. Please, God, let him be all right, she prayed as one of the night staff came over to take Ben's details.

Time seemed to stand still from that point on. She had no idea how long it was before Sean came back, looking infinitely weary but smiling. He took her hands as she stood up unsteadily.

'He's going to be fine, Claire. Do you want to see him?'

'Please.' Her legs felt like jelly as he led her into the familiar room but it felt different, being on the receiving end of treatment for once. Ben was lying on the bed nearest the door and he gave her a wobbly grin as she bent down to kiss him.

'Hi, Mum. Guess I gave you a fright, didn't I?'

'You certainly did! Took years off my life and probably gave me a few more grey hairs,' she replied teasingly. She looked round as Sean joined them. 'Thank you, Sean. I don't know what went wrong tonight and why he had such a severe attack, but I do know that both Ben and I are grateful to you.'

'All part of the job. And as to why he had the attack, I think Ben can explain that himself.' He raised his brows as Ben looked sheepish.

'It was the hamster, Mum.'

'We don't have a hamster,' she replied blankly.

'Um, well, not really we don't. But Danny wanted me to look after his hamster while he's on holiday so I brought it home with me. I was playing with it in bed tonight,' he explained.

'Benedict Shepherd, how many times do I have to tell you that you must be careful about playing with furry animals!' Claire began, but Sean cut in quickly, giving Ben a conspiratorial wink.

'I'm sure he's sorry, Claire. And he's promised that he won't do it again, haven't you, young man?' he asked, looking sternly at the little boy, who wriggled uncomfortably.

'Uh-huh.'

'So I think we can safely assume that he's learnt his lesson.' Sean looked round as Mike Kennedy came into the room. 'I'm going to take Claire for a cup of tea, Mike. Will you keep an eye on Ben? He'll be going up to the children's ward once they've sorted out a bed...purely as a precaution,' he added, sensing Claire's alarm. 'He'll be as right as rain by the morning, you'll see.'

'As long as he doesn't go fostering any more homeless hamsters,' Claire said drily, making them all laugh.

She let Sean lead her away as Ben settled down to rest, knowing that the best thing for him now was to get some sleep. She felt worn out herself, still shaken by the thought of what might have happened if Sean hadn't been able to get Ben's breathing under control.

A shiver rippled through her, followed by another and another as reaction set in. Sean muttered something under his breath as he led her to the relatives' room and sat her down, sitting beside her to chafe her cold hands between his.

'He's fine, Claire. Honestly. You know as well as I do that once the attack is over that's it.'

'I know that. I just can't help thinking what might have happened, though…'

'But it didn't. So stop torturing yourself. I know it's easy for me to say because he isn't my son, but I can imagine how it feels, Claire.'

There was a wealth of sadness in his voice, a pain which cut her to the quick to hear. She looked into his eyes and saw the shadows that dulled them, and suddenly she knew that she couldn't stay silent any longer. It was too important that Sean know the truth, no matter what repercussions it caused.

She drew her hands away and stood up, needing to set a little distance between them. 'I have something I need to tell you, Sean, something important about Ben. I'm not sure how you're going to take it, though. All I can say is that what I did was with the very best of intentions. You see, Ben is—'

'Dr Fitzgerald?' Louise Graham, the staff nurse on duty that night, popped her head round the door, grimacing as she saw Claire. 'Oops, sorry. Didn't mean to interrupt, but we've got an ambulance on its way in. Man who's fallen through a pub window and suffered severe lacerations.'

'I'll be right there, Louise. Thanks.' He turned back

to Claire as the door closed. 'I'm sorry but I'll have to go. Will it keep till later?'

She nodded numbly, struck by the sheer irony of the situation. She had kept her secret for eight long years so a few more minutes weren't going to make much difference!

Sean frowned, obviously sensing something from her expression. 'This is important, isn't it, Claire? And it's about Ben—' He broke off as the blare of a siren announced the arrival of the ambulance. His face was a picture of indecision as he was torn between a desire to hear what she had to say and a need to attend to the incoming patient.

'You go and do what needs to be done, Sean,' she said softly. 'What I have to tell you will keep a bit longer.'

'Are you going to stay here tonight with Ben?' he asked, already moving towards the door. 'Then I'll come and find you when I'm through here,' he added when she nodded. Then he hurriedly left.

Claire followed him out into the corridor, watching as he hurried after the stretcher, which was just disappearing into the trauma room. She made her way to the lift and pressed the button for the third floor. Ben had been put in a side room to avoid waking up the rest of the children and he was sound asleep.

Claire stood by his bed, feeling her love for him welling up inside her. This was Sean's son, the product of their love. For Ben's sake…for all their sakes…she had to find the right way to tell Sean the truth because it mattered so much that he accepted it!

CHAPTER ELEVEN

'RIGHT, there should be everything you need in the bathroom—soap, shampoo, even some of those disposable toothbrushes. Oh, and I found this for you to wear. Not the most glamorous of outfits but at least it's better than those pyjamas!'

Rachel Hart, the staff nurse on the children's ward, grinned as she laid a pale green scrub suit on the bed. Claire smiled her thanks, appreciating the trouble the other woman had gone to on her behalf.

It had been Rachel's suggestion that she use the family suite attached to the ward to freshen up after a night spent at Ben's bedside. Sean still hadn't been to see her but she had heard several ambulances coming in and realised that he must have been too busy to get away. It didn't help her increasing nervousness, however. Now that she had made her decision she wanted to get everything over and done with!

'These are great, Rachel,' she said, trying to stop herself worrying about what she was going to say when the time came. 'It's a good idea, having this suite here. Must make it easier for the parents if they need to stay any length of time with their children.'

'It's been a godsend,' Rachel replied fervently, looking round the comfortably furnished bed-sitter. 'Before the League of Friends raised the money for it, any parents wanting to stay overnight had to camp out in the waiting-room, which was hardly ideal. Anthea Berry has been using it for the past couple of weeks but she finally decided to go home now that Simon is making such good progress. Anyway, take your time and don't worry about Ben. We'll let him sleep as long as he wants. It's the best thing after an asthma attack like that.'

Rachel hurried back to the ward. Breakfasts were being served so it was a busy time for all the staff supervising the youngsters. Claire took a long, hot shower then dressed in the fresh clothes, thankfully stowing her nightclothes into a plastic carrier she found in a drawer.

Leaving the bag on the bed, she went to see if Ben was awake. He had slept peacefully all night long, obviously worn out by what had happened to him. He was still fast asleep when she pushed open the door and was oblivious to the man who was standing by the bed, looking at him with an expression of such longing on his face that it stole her ability to move. It was only as Sean turned to look at her that she managed to take the last couple of steps into the room.

'He hasn't woken up yet, then, I take it?'

Sean's voice was level enough but it couldn't conceal the undercurrent of emotion she heard in the deep tones. Claire took a quick breath but her heart was hammering so fast that it seemed hard to breathe.

'No. Rachel said that they were going to leave him to sleep as long as he wants to,' she replied in a voice which was little more than a whisper.'

Sean nodded. 'Best thing for him. He gave you a real fright last night, didn't he, Claire? That must be the downside of having a child, the fact that you worry about them so much. But I imagine there's plenty to make up for it.'

He knew! Claire had no idea how she knew that but she did. Sean knew that Ben was his son and was simply waiting for her to confirm it.

She clasped her hands together to stop them trembling but she could feel the way her whole body was shaking. Would he be angry with her? Would he resent what she had done so much that he would try to…to take Ben away from her?

Fear rushed through her in a great wave so that she couldn't speak. She had a cowardly urge to simply turn tail and run, rather than face what was to come.

'Tell me, Claire…please!'

The entreaty in his voice brought her eyes to his face and her fear evaporated. This was Sean she was about to entrust with her secret. Wasn't he the most caring, compassionate, *loving* man she had ever met? What did she have to fear from him? Suddenly it was easy.

'Ben is your son, Sean. What I told everyone about his father was a lie.' She looked straight at him, wanting there to be no doubt in his mind that she was telling him the truth. 'You are Ben's father.'

He closed his eyes and she saw the tremor that ran through him. 'Thank you, Claire. Thank you from the bottom of my heart, even though I don't deserve this!'

He opened his eyes and held his arms out to her. She gave a small cry of relief as she ran into them, crying unashamedly as he held her close.

'Shh, don't cry, sweetheart. This is a time for rejoicing, not crying.' He lifted her chin and kissed away her tears, although his own eyes were misty. 'It isn't every day you learn you're a father.'

'How did you guess?' she whispered huskily.

'Because I suddenly realised as I was standing here that you couldn't possibly have done what I accused you of.' He lifted her face and looked deep into her eyes. 'You just wouldn't have slept with anyone else when you were seeing me, which left me with just one answer as to who Ben's father was. I…I just needed to hear you say it.'

'And you…you don't hate me for not telling you?' she said hesitantly.

'I could never hate you, Claire. Oh, I tried to when I thought you'd deceived me, but even then I couldn't manage it.'

He drew her even closer, as though he needed to feel her near him at that moment. 'These past weeks have been pure hell. I couldn't even trust myself to speak to you because I was afraid that I'd end up making an even bigger fool of myself if I did.'

'What do you mean?' she asked, frowning up at him.

He smoothed away the frown lines with his lips, smiling as she shivered. 'That I probably would have ended up telling you how I felt, that I was still crazy about you.' He shrugged. 'Believing that you were still in love with someone else, I knew how foolish *that* would have been!'

'But there isn't anyone else!' She smiled into his eyes. 'There never has been. The only man I've ever loved is you, Sean. You said once that no one could match up to Ben's father in my eyes and you were right, even though you didn't realise exactly what you were saying at the time!'

'Oh, Claire…darling!' His mouth was hungry as it settled over hers, but the kiss was destined to be far too brief as a familiar voice suddenly piped up.

'Why are you and Sean kissing, Mum? Does it mean you two like each other?'

Claire went bright pink with embarrassment as she realised that Ben was wide awake and watching them with interest. Sean grinned as he loosened his hold on her, although he still kept his arm around her.

'I think you could say that, Ben. Your mum and I happen to like each other very much. Is that all right with you?'

'Yeah, course it is.' Ben replied nonchalantly. 'I s'pose you're going to get married now? Peter Baxter said that his mum and his new dad were *always* kissing before they got married. Yuk!'

Sean laughed deeply as he ruffled the boy's hair. 'Yuk, indeed. As to whether or not your mum will marry me depends on you. How would you feel about me being your dad, Ben?'

Claire held her breath as she waited to hear what the child would say. Would Ben like the idea? Or would he resent someone else coming into their lives?

'Depends,' Ben muttered, staring down at the coverlet on the bed.

'On what?' Sean queried gently, squeezing Claire's hand as he felt her tense.

'On whether or not you'll be a real dad—you know, taking me fishing and playing football and things. Peter said that his new dad is always too tired to play with him,' he added by way of explanation.

Sean took a deep breath but Claire could hear the relief in his voice. 'I promise you that I shall be a *real* dad in every way possible, Ben. Although, of course, that does mean nagging you about doing your homework and tidying your room and—'

'OK!' Ben laughed, realising that Sean was teasing him. 'I've always wanted a dad so I don't suppose it will be *that* bad!'

Sean smiled at the boy with such tenderness that it brought a lump to Claire's throat. 'No, I don't suppose it will. In fact, I'm looking forward to it. Mind you, I'm jumping the gun a bit because I haven't asked your mum yet how she feels about the idea.'

He looked round as a nurse appeared with Ben's breakfast. He waited until she had gone before turning to the boy again, speaking this time in a conspiratorial tone.

'I'm going to whisk your mum away for half an hour to see if I can persuade her. Is that all right with you?'

'No problemo,' Ben replied in his best imitation of one of his screen heroes. He was happily tucking into his breakfast as Sean and Claire left the room.

Claire's head was reeling at the speed with which things were moving as she led the way to the family suite. She closed the door and turned to Sean, gasping as he pulled her unceremoniously into his arms and kissed her soundly.

He let her go and his eyes were full of tenderness as he saw her bemused expression. 'We have eight years to make up for, Claire, so I'm not going to apologise for rushing things.'

She gave a shaky laugh as she drew his head down and kissed him. 'Don't you think we should get things straight first, though? You have no idea why I never told you about Ben, for starters.'

He led her over to the bed-settee and sat down, his arm going around her to hold her close. 'No? Oh, I think I can work it out, Claire, now that I'm thinking straight for the first time in ages.'

He tilted her face so that he could look deep into her eyes. 'You were afraid that I would refuse to go to Africa if I knew you were pregnant, weren't you? You knew how much I wanted to go there and you didn't want me to feel that I had to give up all my dreams.'

She gave him a gentle smile, surprised by how *un-*

surprised she felt that he had guessed her reasons. 'Yes. I knew that I couldn't possibly go with you in the circumstances and that you would never leave me once you found out about the baby. I was terrified that at some point in the future you would come to hate me and maybe hate Ben because he was the reason you'd had to change all your plans.'

'How could you think I'd ever feel like that?' There was no denying the shock in his voice, and she grimaced.

'Because I'd seen it happen at first hand. My own parents married because my mother was expecting me. My father once told me that it was all my fault that he hadn't done the things he'd wanted to. I was only a child at the time but I…I never forgot it.'

'What a dreadful thing to say to any child! It's so cruel and so untrue.' Sean brushed her mouth with a tender kiss and she could tell how deeply affected he was by what she'd told him.

'So you decided that rather than run that risk you would face the future alone?' An expression of intense pain crossed his face when she nodded. 'I could never have hated you, my love, or resented Ben. Not for any reason!'

She swallowed the lump in her throat, knowing that he meant it. 'I can see that now but at the time I was so scared. I loved you so much, Sean, that I simply couldn't take the risk. It would have destroyed me if you'd come to hate me and seen our child as a burden.'

'Oh, darling!' He rained kisses over her face, murmuring tender little endearments as he soothed away her fears. Claire snuggled closer, drawing comfort from the feel of his arms around her so that it was easier to explain when he prompted her to continue.

'Why did you tell Ben that his father was dead? You must have had a very good reason for that, darling.'

'I did, or so I thought.' She sighed. 'Again, it was because of what had happened to me, I'm afraid. I didn't want Ben to spend his life waiting for you to turn up and feeling rejected when you didn't.'

She shrugged. 'As you know, my parents divorced when I was ten. After that I hardly ever saw my father. Oh, he kept promising to come and see me but he never did. I used to spend hours sitting by the window, waiting for him. It simply reinforced the idea of how little he cared about me. I didn't want Ben to go through that. For his sake, I had to cut you out of our lives completely.'

'And all that time you struggled to bring Ben up on your own. That's something I shall never forgive myself for, that I wasn't there to help you.' His voice broke and he drew her to him, nuzzling his face into her hair. 'When I came back to England I tried my very best to find you.'

'You did?' She couldn't hide her surprise.

'Yes. I'd never really got over you, you see.' He shrugged ruefully. 'I told myself that if I could just see you again, maybe I could finally put what we'd had behind me. I think I was half hoping that I'd discover that you were happily married because that would have meant there was no chance at all of us ever getting back together.'

'Oh, Sean!' She kissed him quickly, her heart aching at what he had gone through.

He gave her a tender smile, his eyes full of love. 'It probably wouldn't have worked, I have to confess, but that was the plan. Anyway, I couldn't find any trace of you, as it happened. Nobody had heard from you after you'd left Sheffield.'

'I deliberately cut all ties,' she confessed quietly. 'I couldn't take the chance of anyone finding out about Ben and maybe telling you. I moved to Manchester and got a job there, before coming to work here. I thought it was the best thing to do.'

'So you didn't even have any friends to help you when you were pregnant?' He groaned deeply as he pulled her back into his arms, and she felt the shudder that ran through his body. It was several minutes before he let her go and there was a wariness about him all of a sudden which made her heart race.

'So, where do we go from here, Claire? Now that I know Ben is my son I want to be with him, but I don't want you agreeing to anything for the wrong reasons.'

'What do you mean?' she asked, puzzled by the sudden flatness of his tone.

'I know that I told Ben just now that we were going to get married but maybe I was a bit hasty.' He stood up abruptly, walking to the window before coming back to stand in front of the settee, and she could see the tension in the rigid set of his shoulders.

'I never asked you what you wanted, Claire. Now I am. Do you want to marry me and, if so, why? Is it just because of Ben? Or—'

'Oh, definitely *or*, Sean!' She laughed as she stood up. 'I love you, Sean. I can't think of anything I want more than to marry you. Is that clear enough?'

'As crystal!' His arms fastened around her so tightly that the breath whooshed from her body. They were so engrossed in one another that they didn't hear the door opening as Rachel popped into the room to see if they needed anything. She quietly backed out again, smiling ruefully to herself. Who said that scrub suits were passion-killers!

They had little time on their own for the rest of the day after they took Ben home. He seemed very excited at the prospect of Sean becoming his father, although Claire was aware that they were going to have to handle the situation carefully. However, as Sean pointed out, there was no rush to tell Ben the truth until they were sure he could cope with it.

Finally, worn out by all the excitement, Ben went to bed. The hamster had been temporarily moved next door to Mrs Mitchell's until other arrangements could be made, and Claire had thoroughly cleaned Ben's bedroom to remove any trace of the animal's fur. She popped in to check on him, putting a finger to her lips as she heard footsteps behind her.

'He's just dropped off,' she warned as Sean came quietly into the room and slid his arms around her waist. She shivered as he nuzzled her neck and she heard him laugh huskily under his breath. Suddenly, the atmosphere in the room seemed to change in the blink of an eye. When he captured her hand and led her towards the door, she went without a murmur.

He stopped on the landing to kiss her slowly, hungrily, smiling down into her face with eyes full of love. 'I think our son has the right idea, my sweet. How about making an early night of it ourselves?'

She shivered at the note of passion in his voice. 'Th-that sounds like a good idea,' she replied huskily.

'Doesn't it just?' Sean's smile was tender as he dropped a kiss on the tip of her nose before he led her into her bedroom.

Claire stepped into his arms, feeling her love for him filling her heart and soul. 'I love you, Sean Fitzgerald.'

'And I love you, Claire Shepherd, although the last part of your name is going to change very soon, I hope.'

He kissed her lingeringly so that they were both breathless when they drew apart. Sean framed her face between his hands, smiling at her with eyes full of love and longing. 'How soon can I make an honest woman of you? One week…two…no more than three maximum!'

'Three weeks? But, Sean, we can't make all the arrangements that quickly,' she protested.

He silenced her the most effective way possible, with a hungry kiss, so that she was trembling when he drew back. 'Of course we can! We can do anything we want to, Claire, as long as we do it together—you, me and Ben.'

Her eyes misted with tears as he drew her back into his arms. 'Yes,' she whispered. 'Yes, you're right. Now that we are a real family nothing is impossible.'

EPILOGUE

TWO weeks and one day later Claire and Sean were married. As she walked down the aisle on Dr Hill's arm, Claire marvelled that everything had gone so smoothly. In fact, there hadn't been a single hitch in making the arrangements.

She had found the perfect dress—rich, creamy-coloured lace with long sleeves and a slim-fitting skirt—in the first shop she'd visited. That had been an omen because from there on everything had simply flowed, from booking the church to arranging the reception. It was as though fate were smiling on her and Sean to make up for how long they'd had to wait for this moment to arrive.

Now, as he turned to watch her coming down the aisle, Claire felt her heart spill over with love as she saw the expression on his face. That Sean loved her was in no doubt to everyone present—all their friends and Sean's family. She passed the row where Sarah Gillespie and her husband, Niall, were sitting, and tried not to chuckle out loud as Sarah winked at her. Sarah had been right because all it had needed in the end had been a bit of courage.

There were a lot of the staff there—Margaret and Janet, Mike Kennedy and his girlfriend amongst a host of others. Sean was well liked at the hospital, and now that he had accepted the senior registrar's post in A and E, which had been vacant for some time, they would be staying in the area.

Claire was glad because she loved Dalverston, but she knew that it would have made no difference where he had decided to work because she would have gone with him. They were meant to be together and nothing was going to stop that happening now!

She stopped beside him at last, feeling warmth encompass her as he took her hand then turned to wink at Ben, who was proudly acting as her page-boy. When Sean motioned for the child to stand beside them at the altar while they made their vows, it just seemed to sum everything up.

From this point on it would be the three of them together...unless there were any future additions, of course!

Claire smiled as Sean slid the slim gold band onto her finger. Maybe they should think about that in the near future, a new little brother or sister—for Ben's sake.

Sensual Romance™
4 brand new titles each month
...teasing, tempting, provocatively playful.
Available on subscription every month from the Reader Service™
GEN/21/RS3

Medical Romance™
6 brand new titles each month
...pulse-rasing romance – heart-racing medical drama
Available on subscription every month from the Reader Service™
GEN/03/RS3

Tender Romance™
6 brand new titles each month
...sparkling, emotional, feel-good romance
Available on subscription every month from the Reader Service™
GEN/02/RS3